THE SWING ERA

SARAH SHEARD

ALFRED A. KNOPF CANADA

PUBLISHED BY ALFRED A. KNOPF CANADA

Copyright © 1993 by Sarah Sheard

All rights reserved under International and
Pan-American Copyright Conventions.
Distributed by Random House of Canada Limited, Toronto.

First Edition

Canadian Cataloguing in Publication Data

Sheard, Sarah.
The swing era

ISBN 0-394-22731-X

1. Title.

PS8587.H4S9 1993   C813'.54   C92-095124-4
PR9193.3.S54S9 1993

Printed and bound in Canada

Toronto, New York, London, Sydney, Auckland

Special thanks to Margaret Atwood, Carole Corbeil,
Louise Dennys, Gillian Kerr, Anne Michaels, Sue Murphy,
Barbara O'Kelly, Michael Ondaatje and David Young
for their insights and careful readings

∽

To V and H for walking me to the promised land

∽

To the Canada Council for a B Grant, the Ontario Arts Council for
a work-in-progress grant and writers' reserve assistance, and to the
City of Toronto for its support through the Toronto Arts Council

∽

An excerpt appeared in *Malahat Review*, Spring, 1990, and in
Ounce of Cure, edited by Mark Anthony Jarman

∽

The scars of others should teach us caution.

– ST. JEROME –

For Benn Dashiell Joseph

⌒

My mother hadn't always been unwell.

I still carry the photos with me of my eighth birthday. She'd spent days preparing a treasure hunt, writing out clues, hiding them in nooks and crannies throughout the house, recording their locations on a clipboard. We had both dressed thematically for that occasion — she in pirate bandanna, earrings, a charcoal moustache, I with cutlass jammed into the sash of my party dress. Dressing up was a game she and I had loved to play at first. It had only been make-believe back then.

The children arriving at our door seemed not to notice anything unusual about my mother who, moustache and all, was beautiful, her shoulder-length hair spilling into her eyes as she bent over each guest, taking coats, distributing the first clues with a wink at me, her co-conspirator, that brought a rush of almost unbearable pride to my heart. The children listened, wide-eyed, to her theatrical warnings about the crocodile under the stairs, the snakes in the attic, gasped when she unveiled the cake she'd made—a map of Port Airedale impeccably rendered in coloured icing, the turrets of our house clearly recognizable, Belvedere Park behind, the winding hill downtown, Hart River, the Sound, our school—all there, even a sailboat tacking into harbour. My father's snapshots caught the children's faces swept with wonder, as at watching a cat giving birth, the cake just below frame.

In their eyes I read delight and envy. They wished she could have been their mother too.

The camera framed my mother and me inside a moment of perfect happiness, cheek to cheek, the flash glinting off the compass pinned to my chest, a treasure she'd planted specially for me to find, whose weight and coolness I can still feel in my hand despite the river of other birthdays that has scoured memory clean.

When its case was flipped open, the blue-tipped needle would flutter and bob, ambivalent at first, as though unwilling to point, *it's rude to point!* yet given a moment to settle on its holder's palm, would swing around and around and then wobble back towards home: True North, this way.

I had wanted, for the longest time, to be a priest or a monk when I grew up, coveting the robes, somewhat like those Jesus might have worn, the cross at my waist like a tiny sword warding off sin and the chaotic materialism of the world. In my monastic cell, one facecloth, one blanket, a narrow bed beneath a window, I would be able to tread out my own path, in contemplative, serene footfalls. No anger, no stress, no fear.

No madness.

When I discovered that girls could not become priests I swallowed my rage and disappointment and announced to my parents I would be a nun instead, although it was very much a second choice. My father told me nunneries were prisons for women of low IQ, which discouraged me terribly—I intended to live a life of the mind. To make amends, he built me a prie-dieu so I could kneel and pray privately in my bedroom whenever I wished, or read from my Bible, a white leather job my mother had given me, that closed with a zipper, like my mouth when I swore to keep a secret.

I memorized the catechism and was confirmed at the age of ten, the youngest in my group. I still have the dress my mother sewed me. I keep everything.

I joined the church altar guild—chars for Christ, my father called them, to my mother's consternation—older ladies who freshened the flowers and vacuumed up the crumbs under the Lord's table. My mother ironed a fresh white blouse for me to wear every Saturday morning, although it hardly seemed logical to dress up only to spend the morning on my hands and knees polishing smudges off the brass chancel rail in preparation for new smudges the following day.

You are in the Lord's House, she said. He sees the little sparrow fall. Wear a clean shirt.

Brass work was the pretext for me to flip open the little latch on the rail gate and slip through, to savour the Shepherd's side of things for a moment, leave flock status behind as I furtively tested the seat in the bishop's stall, turned to face the altar under the mournful gaze of Christ in stained glass, his own heart bleeding in his hand.

On Sunday mornings from my family pew near the front I would lose myself in the painted folds of His ruby mantle, long to hold His impeccably shod foot in both my hands. I would have given my eyes to visit Galilee in a time machine, hear Him talk, perform miracles, like that of the woman who'd haemorrhaged for twelve years, pushing through the crowd to touch the hem of His robe and be cured. He had turned, feeling the power draw off Him, voltage enough to cure anyone, even my mother. Your faith has made you whole, He had said, modestly declining credit.

The chars for Christ were responsible for the Communion linen and the priest's robes, kept locked in the vestry. The chasuble, a heavily embroidered vestment worn like a poncho over the surplus and cassock, had to be selected and laid out depending on the feast day: white for Christmas, purple for Lent and so on. The keys to the vestry wardrobe were entrusted to me, and it was my particular pleasure to lift the heavy silks out, hang them in the priest's changing closet next door and return the previously worn robes to the wardrobe.

The chasubles were awkward and long. Even slung across both arms there was the risk of wrinkling, with no place to lay them down while unlocking the wardrobe, so it seemed only efficacious for me to slip them on instead while walking from one chamber to the other, struggling with the keys.

The other chars were invariably down in the kitchen brewing tea by this time and ironing up the last of the linen—until the one regrettable day when I must have taken too long and they came upstairs in search of me.

They swung open the vestry door, all unsuspecting, and startled me into turning, both arms upraised in priestly vestments, as though to bless them. I was only reaching to push shut the linen drawer—but too late.

It had also upset them that certain of my fingers were folded in the signature gesture used by our rector in imitation of Christ, which I don't recall doing although I will admit to having blocked much of that episode.

I surrendered the vestry keys and walked for the last time down those linoleum steps the colour of overdone roast beef, past the saloon doors of the washroom with the pressure taps that sprang back when the hand released them, *waste not, want not,* past the ancient radiator pipes taped like limbs in traction that carried the clang and bang of the boiler up into the pulpit itself, the Body of Christ so overheated in winter the paint flaked off in curls and the choirboys swooned in their stalls, past the warped stacks of plum-coloured Books of Common Prayer, the varnished oak tract boxes secured with a doll's padlock, below the hanging lights shaped like shields in opaque butterscotch glass, speckled with dead flies, the windows set so high they caught the dappled reflection of trees and were pulled open by servers with pikestaffs, out the fortress doors of studded wood and into the din of the outside world.

I needed to talk to my mother badly. I was crying by the time I got home, but the house was empty, the car gone. Three hours later there was still no sign of them and it was past dinnertime. He must have taken her for another doctor's appointment. In too much of a hurry, obviously, to have left me a note. I'd begged them, after the last time, please to leave me one.

I made myself a cold supper, went out back and climbed up into my tree to watch for their car. The stars were visible against the sky. They were always forgetting about me now that she was sick or else telling me what to do, ordering me out of the room like a dog they didn't want.

I studied the inside of my wrist where two little rivers,

thin and blue as pen marks, flowed up over the joint then disappeared into the thicker skin of my palm. The Tigris or the Euphrates. Which one would it be today? With my pocketknife I nicked the left vein and then touched to it what I'd stolen that afternoon from the rectory cupboard—a priest's Host that turned redder than a harvest moon and dissolved into a foam I licked off, and then I soaked another one and ate that too and then another until they were all gone, and then I stretched out on my branch to wait for the car, listening to the drops fall from my wrist onto the leaves below like the drops of sweat in Gethsemane.

My mother's psychiatrist admitted to me the possibility of a hereditary factor, having also treated my maternal grandmother for a similar dysfunction. I told him I was afraid, particularly of having a child, especially a daughter, that I'd heard the stress and hormones of pregnancy could trigger its onset, that my grandmother's and my mother's illness had begun in their thirties, that my grandmother's hands were carbon copies of my mother's hands and of my hands as well. Their eyes, my eyes.

The doctor warned me that worrying was the worst thing to do, that I had years to go before thinking about having a child. He encouraged me to continue my studies, avoid drugs, get adequate sleep, keep track of my dreams, try not to imagine symptoms.

I decided to believe him, as susceptible as my mother to bouts of wishful thinking.

Nepal. Five years later.

Kapok. The cottony fluff was so dry it made me shiver. I sniffed it. Faint trace of the odour of life preservers, mildewed, like those in my canoe back home. I reached into the sack, took out another handful and stuffed it into the meditation cushion until it was full and could be stitched closed. I counted the cushions yet to be finished. Sewing had never been my strong suit.

Surely, tea must be coming soon. I cocked an ear for the rattle of the cart across the stones of the courtyard. Sometimes the acolytes forgot me in their rounds, presuming the shrine hall to be empty this time of day.

The temple gong was struck. End of afternoon work period.

I stacked the finished cushions inside the wooden cupboard at the back of the hall, bowed to the shrine figure, closed the double doors behind me and went outside, picking my way carefully around the perimeter of the kitchen garden to wash up outside Main House where we slept and ate.

In the corridor a young acolyte was on his hands and knees wiping down the planks ahead of me, drying a section immediately after wetting it so as not to cause a hazard to others. My first days at the temple had been occupied with tasks such as this, concentrating all my energy and attentiveness on their perfect execution, dispelling the almost hourly spasms of rage and despair I had brought with me from home. I wondered what private demons this young man was banishing as he worked.

I found Panchen in the kitchen, the only monk who spoke sufficient English to act as translator for me when I first arrived. Now that I had undertaken a six-month vow of silence we had to communicate by signs. He smiled and bowed, revealing a generous mouth and perfect teeth, youthful features in spite of years of ascetic life. Minding the kitchen was soft retirement for him compared to his years of outdoor labour. His easy smile and playful nature— as rare as meat in this temple—endeared him to me.

He was sifting rice in a barrel, picking through for stones and husks. "Some, how-you-say, thief I got, walking around kitchen at night, stealing barley, stealing butter, stealing dried fruits." He looked sidelong at me. "Maybe thief is you."

I thumped my chest in mock horror and shook my head. I was desperate, however, for something to eat, a standing joke between us. I simply could not adjust to the eternity that passed between temple meals, the meagre portions and the strangeness of some of the food. I made my usual signs, begging theatrically and plucking at his cuff.

He pretended not to notice.

I clapped my hands. A gesture that had to be respected from one who had undertaken my vow.

He rubbed his face, pretending to consider, then reached into a barrel, turned and stretched out two closed fists. I tapped the right. An apple.

Occasionally I lost and he would only shrug and put the treat back. Everything was training. Everyone here was a beginner, Teacher said, including himself.

I finished my apple, put the core in the compost barrel, bowed to it and—*clack!* The wooden claves were struck outside, announcing the start of evening meditation. Instantly the corridor began filling with monks and nuns, selected laity and acolytes, shuffling as one through the double doors of the shrine room, bowing and making prostrations, arranging themselves on their cushions beneath the gaudy hanging tapestries that gave the hall an illusion of warmth, tugging their robes straight, giving their shoulders and necks a roll before the final gong sounded that would put an end to all further movement.

Teacher came in last and took his place on the dais beside the senior lama, his former teacher, a dessicated old bird, whose occasional attacks of musical flatulence during evening meditation provoked spasms of stifled laughter among the novices.

Teacher nodded to the monitor to pick up his little hand bell.

As the tinkling died away the hall fell motionless, not a twitch among the rows of bodies, seated, spines erect, heads slightly inclined, eyes fixed at a spot on the floor in front of them. The lama was already sunk deep in meditation, a living statue, his breathing audible in the silence of the great hall.

I had often wanted to watch his face as he settled in, curious to observe him enter the deeper stages of meditation but my slightest movement would have been bound to attract the notice of the sitters around me.

I was sitting observing my own thought-stream, doing my best to avoid distraction, when suddenly the floor creaked and my concentration wobbled. A stutter of voices from back home rose up, my mother's crazy laughter in the middle of the night, my father calling for me to help, the ambulance pulling up.

I began to rock from side to side on my cushion....

The monitor scurried up the row from behind, brandishing Teacher's encouragement stick, a flat baton of mountain ash. He touched my back to warn me, then delivered three stinging blows to each shoulder and the visions flew out of me with a rush, the floor rolling up to meet me—I would have fallen had the monitor not clamped a steadying hand to my shoulder and held it there until my head cleared and I was able to raise my folded hands in the gesture of thanks. He moved on with a rustle of robes and I tried to settle back down but my concentration was in tatters.

It hadn't been easy to get to this place. Travelling alone through Nepal had been difficult at times: the water, the terrain, the climate, the altitude, wild dogs and monkeys, disease-carrying mosquitoes. Once I'd arrived, it took some time to get admitted to the temple itself. I had to make numerous applications to local and government authorities to extend my visa, meanwhile performing traditional proofs of sincerity by sitting in meditation outside the temple gate in the cold rain, day after day, all in vain, until finally, one miraculous morning, everything came together. I was helped to my feet, handed a piece of paper stamped with an official seal and led, hobbling, inside for an interview with Teacher, translating through Panchen. Later I discovered that Teacher could, in fact, speak quite good English on his own.

My father wrote, asking did I have the freedom to come and go as I pleased and were they pressuring me to pledge money to them?

I sent back a Polaroid of my new self, shorn and robed, my sunburned cherry nose in my western face explaining that my money meant nothing to them—or to me any more. I was learning how to live moment to moment, free of anger and anxiety. I'd been sprung from Sing Sing. Be happy for me, Dad, I wrote. At last, eighteen months later, I was beginning to feel stirrings of hope, my old skin shed, a new one growing, leading a serene and anonymous life here.

Until this visitation. Self-pity welled up. Halfway around the world to escape—in vain. I was about to burst out crying in the meditation hall. What was this? Dissolving dualism with tears?

The bell tinkled. End of meditation. I wiped my face with my cuff as we stood and bowed, knelt and rearranged our cushions before filing past the gilt figure of the Buddha to make our final prostrations and leave the hall for supper.

For the past hour I've been waiting in my room with soap and towel, listening to the new arrivals shuffle up and down the hall in one-size-fits-none sandals we all wear, opening and closing doors, exchanging protracted goodnights with one another. Three of them are Americans, mountain trekkers, whose presence I resent intensely, together with their volumes of small talk and reluctance to adapt to temple routines, their eagerness to impart news of the outside world, presuming I must be starved for what I called their global gossip—although I had to admit their cassettes of rock music were delicious, listened to through new-style headphones so minimal they nestled inside the ear like pills.

When all fell quiet I gathered up my bath things and slipped into the corridor, wrapping my privacy around me, hoping not to run into anyone.

The hall was deserted. Just as I had passed the last door, it swung open and one of the trekkers, a Swiss, naked from the waist up, glanced out at me. He was obviously expecting someone else. I had grown accustomed to inhabiting a neutral zone of my body, especially here in this dormitory of dwellers who had likewise surrendered sexual expression in their quest for something beyond. In the instant that passed between us I read recognition, first of his mistake, then of my femaleness, a look of bald appraisal that had not been there earlier at supper.

Flustered, I held up my bath things to indicate my mission and he smiled and stepped back, releasing me. The click of his door and the geriatric shuffling of my own slippers filled me with melancholy. I locked myself in the bathroom and hung up my robe—loathing my naked body, scarred and mottled in the mirror above the sink.

Prune face. Twenty-two years old and already I looked ancient. I leaned into the mirror and mouthed: *Dog meat.*

The meditation bell tinkled in Teacher's hand.

We tied our jackets, rose and rearranged our cushions, the movements mechanical and economic with practice. As unobtrusively as possible I shook the pins and needles out of my legs.

The bell rang again. Someone touched my back. I turned and saw it was the monitor. We bowed to one another. He made a gesture indicating that something written had come for me, a telegram it seemed. He pointed down the mountain. I'd done the trip before. Easily an hour's walk downhill to a rope bridge and across it to a shed where supplies, mail and donations from the village were customarily left off.

He pointed to his wrist, meaning I was expected to go immediately although the evening meal was about to be prepared. When he saw I understood he bowed once more and vanished.

It could only be bad news. Regular mail was distributed on Friday nights. This was Wednesday. I wondered why he hadn't simply brought me the letter himself. I fought an impulse to disobey and walk instead to the kitchen garden, finish my rows of hoeing and watering. Who would take over my job of helping to prepare the evening meal, chopping and salting the vegetables, measuring out the barley? I didn't want to fetch any messages from home.

I set off. The ebbing sun was drawing a curtain of shadow across the valley below, filling it in, bringing the terraced ridge on the far side so close I felt I could step across and walk down. Cloud wrapped itself against the mountain, buffeting my face. Each breath drew its chill deeper into my lungs. I tried to recall what one of the trekkers had said the night before, about using wind, descending on its spine.

Twinge of hunger and now a sharp little stone under my instep. I shook out my sandal and walked on. First wave of fatigue. I'd been up since five. I breathed deeply, exhaled and drove it out. Food again. An image of the meal I was about to miss leaped into my mind and my stomach tightened. *Just observe and let it pass.* Flurry of irritation, then of desires, one after another, for the Swiss trekker's dark nipple, a shot of scotch, a slice of rare roast beef.

Interesting. I walked faster.

The roar of the cataract was audible long before I caught sight of it, the path descending sharply, twisting around boulders and gullies. The rough ground and the quality of light reduced me to a crawl in places. When I finally reached the bridge—an avian weave of wood, rope and wire—I pinched my nostrils and blew to clear out my ears and the water's roar doubled in volume. Halfway across the bridge I stumbled and it bucked under me like a roller-coaster track. I stopped and rode out the after-shocks, giggling in terror as I clung to the ropes.

Once in the shed I could barely make out the mail shelf and the telegram's white tip in the gloom. I took it outside and read:

Your mother passed away March 15, 5:40 p.m. Fatal accident. Memorial service awaiting your immediate return or word otherwise. Much love, Father.

Sometime later, I folded the envelope and stuck it inside my jacket. I was exhausted but too hungry to lie down and sleep.

It was so dark I had to navigate across the bridge this time by touch.

Teacher talked to me the morning I left. A private audience. The sun, perfectly positioned behind him, cast his head in silhouette against the mountains, a gift, the image of his darkened face, the almost imperceptible movements of his mouth as he spoke then fell silent, allowing what he'd just said to sink in. So many important memories for me had been caught in sunlight.

Be awake every moment. You have not yet discovered what you came here for. You think to return now is . . . untimely, but life does not deal accidental cards. Don't waste opportunity. Distractions will divert you.

Other words had followed. Short silences. I observed where his inflections marked a deeper contour of meaning, information he intended specifically for me.

The words he chose were simple, their economy a reflection both of the philosophy and his limited English. Recalling any of his talks, I inevitably reconstituted them with more verbiage than he had used, diluting their essence somewhat. He, the poet, I, a paraphraser. Today I had made an effort, as he spoke, to retain his words exactly, to push them into memory like cloves into an orange, a pomander, making a complex fragrance that would become much more than cloves, an orange, time in a dark space.

Already, much time has passed . . . The monk spread his palms open in a gesture that suggested futility and a stab of fear shot through me. *Who knows how much remains?*

Had he seen something? He folded his hands and narrowed his eyes and I was suddenly afraid the interview was over. I sat flushed with confusion, not caring to conceal it in the hope that he might say just one thing more, clarify himself. His eyes opened and looked intently into mine, resting inside them somewhere, inviting me to exchange this intimacy with him. He seemed not to be asking me any question. When I understood that, I relaxed and surrendered. My pupils widened and my face, the prow of the ship of myself, began to spread like smoke—not a hallucination, I recognized that, having had many of them in the first months of meditation, but an opening out, making transparent what had been opaque—for fear of— I couldn't quite catch it. After a moment I could see quite clearly the aura around the old monk's head, backlit against the snow beyond, could hear birds rustling among the bean plants I'd staked up in the garden below, and the silence between individual sounds—the air itself broken into presence and absence.

These things take time. He clapped his hands, releasing me from my vow of silence. *No matter.*

The seatbelt sign flickered and came on. We were preparing to land at last.

The windy corridor of the airport revived me somewhat. I stepped into the moving sidewalk they'd installed since my departure and dropped my bag to my feet, conscious of the stares I was attracting from the people around me. It was not my height and broad shoulders, work tan and ascetic leanness but my stubbled scalp that was drawing the looks. The western clothes I wore only accentuated the oddness of my appearence and I wondered whether I would actually have been less conspicuous in my monastic robes.

I nudged my bag forward an inch. Fainting was a distinct possibility.

The billowy sensation of the ground beneath me as I stepped off the sidewalk was short-lived but intense even though I was prepared for it. The ground grew firmer with each step as though changing from bog to dry land. I drank a cup of coffee from a thin plastic cup, threw it into a refuse container filled with them and boarded my train. Out my window I watched the city ebb away. The slab construction of malls and industrial development, designed, it seemed, by cars for their own convenience, became more episodic until finally the train was sliding past open pastureland bordered by subdivisions of insect architecture, stacked and cellular, laid in clutches. I fell asleep.

A sharp pain in my neck woke me. My head had fallen into the crevice between my seat and the window, my cheek was wet with drool, and the conductor was swaying over me, waiting to punch my ticket. I wiped my cheek and rummaged in my pocket, wondering how long he'd been standing there. My arm was hot from the sun. The trees were cedar now, an occasional stand of birch, tamarack. My watch, still set at Nepali time, showed I'd been asleep for almost three hours. The train was picking its way through outcroppings of shield, great boulders dripping meltwater that reared up on both sides. It was starting to look more like Port Airedale landscape. What could farmers have been thinking of, trying to plow such thin dirt. Where they'd blasted I could see granite, not more than four inches below the surface. From Port Airedale north to Lake Superior the ground only got worse.

We were hurtling past woods and fields now. The grass was still cropped velvet from its hibernation, olive drab, save where the sun had lingered here and there. Totting up the animals I'd managed to spot along the way, I marvelled at the covert discretion of wildlife: one great blue heron, two groundhogs, some mallards and Canada geese browsing among the blasted stalks of a cornfield. That was all.

We pulled into the outskirts of Port Airedale, shooting past the familiar palisade of firs sheltering the town from the wind that pitted granite and stripped foliage, bent every tree alive into that characteristic, painterly shape. Backyards, exposed to view from the tracks, were left untended, the owners indifferent to judgement from passing strangers. An abandoned car, late sixties model, lay snagged in an undergrowth of copse, a traditional Port Airedale aboveground burial accorded to junk that was too much work to cart away. Stripped and gutted, it had lightened, was skeletal, stranded in those thin branches, dessicated by wind and sun, the paint muted, almost natural now. A lesson that I couldn't make out. I'd been travelling, in a hermetic compartment of one kind or another, most of my life, hurtling past intervals of such landscape, unbreathed, unenterable, at right angles to my own progress from past into future. I'd inherited the linear track, kept to it all this time.

The train slowed down, crept along inexplicably for minutes before finally pulling into the shed-roofed siding. There was a release of brakes and the doors swung open. The air of Port Airedale. Pine gum and sweet water. I filled my lungs and reached my satchel down. My bag had become my companion, invested with feelings paralleling my own. It was tired too, thirsty, relieved to be within sight of home at last.

The open Sound, a twinkling sheet in the distance.

I threw my bag into the back seat of the taxi and slid in beside it. The driver started the engine and craned around for instruction, his meaty hand squeezing the back of the seat.

"Belvedere Street. Cable House. You know it?" I caught myself wanting to use my hands to explain. After nearly three months of silence, talking had stopped coming naturally.

He grinned, showing a lot of gum. "Of course. The circular drive. Nice place."

I slid down exhausted in the seat, the scar on my left hand beginning to throb again where I'd smashed it lifting my bag through a turnstile. Silver flesh, waxy tendons. I began to chant furiously under my breath.

"That's some haircut. You a musician?" He began to riffle through a box of cassettes on the seat beside him, handed me one of a young woman with a Celtic name, her head shorn, eyes as large and frightened as a deer's.

A rosary swung from his rear-view. The Pope waved benignly from the sun visor. A vial of clear liquid was mounted in red velvet on his dash. In Nepal and India I had often found myself in taxis kitted up like shrines with sacred pictures, prayer wheels, deity figurines. I leaned forward and pointed. "You get that in the Holy Land?"

"What? Air freshener?" He scrutinized my face. I turned to look out the window.

We passed one of those aboveground swimming pools that had proliferated now that the installation technology had outsmarted Port Airedale winters. The water was dark with accumulated leaves and muck and I wondered why they hadn't covered it with a tarp. Next door was a scrapyard stacked with broken letters from a supermarket. The distinctive, hollow *D, O, W,* or was it an *M.* Lumber King loomed up ahead, shakes of ply, aging in the yard, pink flesh blackened from the winter's weathering, the planks sagging between their chocks, warped all of a piece. Good for boat hulls maybe.

The driver asked something unintelligible. I shrugged, hoping to get out of it. He grinned and raised his eyebrows, flicked on the radio. A singer came on and the driver turned it up, a ballad about catching a catfish and a woman called Doreen. I liked the voice, nasal, boyish, could see the face that might have belonged to it. Wildebeest features. Mother would have loathed it.

I rolled down my window. Daddy's town, Mummy's town. I hadn't been twenty minutes back inside Port Airedale and already my breathing was getting tight. The thought of seeing my father again, hearing what had happened to her, suffering through his inevitable awkwardness in the telling, made my temples ache. We were so adept at the empty postcard, the newsless letter, at contriving serenity for ourselves inside the storms my mother brought, conversing above the roar, clinking our glasses together benignly as the orchestra slid overboard, playing our little word games: "Straighten up and fly right" I would scold, one of Mother's beloved Andrews Sisters' songs. Or the one that made him guffaw: "Beat me, Daddy, eight to the bar."

What was that I smelled? Resinous heat, my own sweat, the driver's musk, the synthetic interior of the car and something else, peculiar, sharp, like burning rubber on toast.

He cocked his head, studying me in the mirror. "Tintoretto's cooking today. The stack's coming up on your right."

Tintoretto. I'd almost forgotten. The ore smelter flitted by, the letters on its sparkling white stack as fat and friendly as caterpillars. I had left town just as they were finishing construction. Rotten eggs. *Brimstone.*

The car wheeled down Main Street past windows displaying video games and home electronics, violent movie posters, expensive sports equipment, a lottery ticket stand, other signs of new affluence. The bakery had expanded. The bookstore was gone. Potted geraniums, whether real or not, I couldn't tell, swung from the lamp standards. We crept through the intersection clogged with cottagers and American yachters in for the day to restock, turned off the main drag and began winding up Belvedere Hill where the fast-food outlets and service stations gave way to stone walls enclosing landscaped properties, set well back from the road itself.

A moment later, the driver palmed the wheel sharply and the car turned into the circular drive of Cable House. There was a popping of gravel under the tires, then silence.

I was back where I'd begun.

~

My father was standing on the verandah, waiting, and I felt that familiar term-end ache of impatience, coming home from boarding school, to jump from the still-moving car into his arms.

"Frederika! Oh God." His voice was husky. "I missed you."

I embraced him, his shoulders feeling smaller inside his sweater than I remembered. He held me away from him. "Wow."

"You like?" I ran a palm over my scalp.

"It's different." He began to laugh.

I reached for my bag but he pulled it out of my hands and carried it into the house. Over his shoulder: "Fresh coffee's in the kitchen."

There was Armagnac, too, among the half-empty bottles of funeral booze. We sat down and he poured us each a shot. The fragrant burn chased by milky caffeine hit my stomach and I felt a rush of warmth that spread to my limbs, my first drink in two years.

He'd lost weight, looked somewhat fitter. He'd also grown a moustache, which quite transformed him, a move he'd threatened to make for years, and the cardigan he was wearing was violet, a remarkable departure from his usual palette of earth and leaves.

"You're looking good, Dad. You in love or something?"

He pulled a fierce face. "Have some respect."

Our old game. I smiled.

"Maybe it's the moustache. You should have seen me back in March." He ran his fingers through his hair, that familiar stiff-fingered jab he made when distracted. I stopped his hand and brought it to rest on the table between us.

"Frederika, I don't know where to begin."

I squeezed his hand and went to the fridge: a wedge of meat pie, brick of dried-out cheese, pint of whole milk. In the crisper drawer, a steak soaking through its wax paper, one withered iceberg lettuce, various condiment bottles wedged along the door rack. I opened the cupboard above the sink: rolled oats, tomato paste, smoked oysters and crackers. That was all.

He smiled, sheepish now. "I put off shopping until you got here."

"Good thing I didn't lay over in Seattle until Tuesday. Your suits would have stopped fitting."

"The freezer's full of casseroles. People keep dropping things off. As though, without a wife"—he laughed dryly—"I'd starve. When was the last time your mother cooked a meal?"

27

I rolled my eyes, remembering the countless dinners I'd been obliged to cobble together as a kid. I found a puckered apple in a paper bag under the sink, pulled out my clasp knife and cut it into quarters. I slid two over to him. "So what happened?"

He looked out the window into the garden, his eyes darting back and forth as though searching for the right words in the grass. He blinked and I saw sorrow rush into his eyes as he poured himself another drink and knocked it back in two swallows. As I refilled his glass I caught him eyeing the scar on the back of my hand. "Over and done with," I said. "History."

"History," he murmured and closed his eyes for a long moment, then began, haltingly, to reconstruct the events of my mother's death, how he'd come home after work to a darkened house, gone upstairs and found her in the bath. She had apparently stood up without thinking and pulled on the overhead light, dying instantly, according to the coroner's report.

The wiring was old. He'd always meant to fix it.

He broke off talking, his head, bowed in grief, gone completely grey now, its whorled thatch as familiar to me as a field to its farmer, bringing a surge of tenderness I longed to express were it not for the embarrassment it would have caused him.

When he realized, he said, that he was having trouble handling what had happened, he went to Toronto a few times to see a therapist who had also helped him admit his anger at me for what I'd done to myself. His face softened. "I'm sleeping better, allowing myself to admit certain feelings. I understand that's progress."

I hid my astonishment. This from a man who thought therapists were for people like my mother and me. "So tell me what comes next."

He sighed. "I've half a mind to move back to Toronto, set up a little law practice again." He smiled and fell silent, both of us knowing that a man in his sixties would no longer be able to do that.

Something of the heaviness I felt on re-entering the house had been dissipated by our talk and I was lifted back to a simpler present, sitting in my father's kitchen, watching the sunset creep up the trunks of the trees.

I got out the iceberg lettuce, ripped it in half and shook chilly gouts of French dressing over each. "Home cooking," he laughed, and then I heard it catch in his throat as I handed him his plate, both of us feigning hunger for the other's sake. I pushed my lettuce around until it looked as if I'd eaten some and then put down my fork, overcome by fatigue, the funereal smell of the house, the vision of my mother's electrified body crashing back into her bathwater.

Wearily I climbed the long flights of stairs to my bedroom, threw open the balcony doors and fell into bed, wondering whether I would ever be able to fall asleep on such a soft mattress. A minute later I lost consciousness.

When I awoke, moonlight was on my face. I pulled a blanket around me and walked out onto the balcony to watch the sequins shimmering on the bay. On the far side of the world I would have been finishing lunch.

I heard again my father's laugh, how it had tightened into a cough of grief. My eyes pricked. The old man.

The finality of her absence squatted down inside my throat, heavy, unbudgeable. I swallowed hard. I who had once wanted it so badly. I could admit that now. Those melancholy years of living with sickness were at an end. I wondered whether the feelings of bitterness associated with that time would ever dissipate. Her life, short-circuited in this way, hugely intensified the distance that had always been between us.

The *ki-yi-yi* of a new-style police siren like a mechanical coyote echoed up the far side of Belvedere Hill. It gargled off in mid-cry as though seizing prey in its jaws. The abrupt plunge into silence was intense at first, the way a candle blown out momentarily shirrs up the darkness into a fog.

I stood at the bathroom door, trying to imagine how it must have been for her, alone in this room witnessed only by these gleaming tiles, the pedestal sink in which I'd baptized my dolls, the Degas print, up above, of a woman rinsing her hair.

She loved that tub. A Victorian clawfoot she'd bathed in since childhood. Nothing conducts like cast iron, she used to sigh with a wink to me, referring to heat; of course, as she slid under her raft of movie-star bubbles. The taps cast a shadow that still looked to me like a giraffe's head, whose knobby horns I used to wrestle with both hands to release the cascade of hot or cold.

A horn mark had been found scorched into the sole of her foot and a second burn, which could not be explained, on her left hip. A posthumous gasp had drawn several c.c.'s of water into her lungs. Those were the findings.

I kicked off my sandals, climbed into the empty tub and lay down. A swatch of breeze from the window set the light fixture swaying above my head, a tiny circular movement, almost imperceptible, like a pulse through a shirt. I'd always dreaded electricity, had more than once been

31

caught on open water watching it strike trees onshore, dreading its approach. She, on the other hand, had drawn it to herself. Her shock therapy, she told me once, with a sufferer's triumph, made a hissing noise in her ears, like tires on a wet night, and a light that flared like a struck match. Those were her words. The doctor said that under sedation it was impossible to register such sensations, but I mistrusted him for dismissing her pain with such authority.

What had been her experience of death? A warm darkness glowing with embers of consciousness that faded eventually to black, the soul guided out of the body towards the flickering light of rebirth? This was an Eastern concept of death, and of natural death at that, but I hoped that some of it could have applied to my mother.

Rosewater. Her bath oil. I caught a trace of it on my fingers and closed my eyes. I could no longer reassemble the features of her face. Her right eye, her mouth parting in a caw of laughter, a marcelled lock of hair, the aristocratic cleft above her lip—each persistently floated out of frame.

The cool walls of the tub loomed up around me like a crib.

Had she wanted me ever? Prayed: *Please, oh Father, cause a daughter to enter my belly.* Cold comfort knowing, when she had gone to such lengths to escape mothering me. I'd tried so hard not to resent her madness personally and now her death. Tried hard to escape from thoughts of her entirely.

I stared into the idiotic bulb of the light fixture that had killed her, its miraculously undamaged shade and the faint telltale ring scorched onto the ceiling that my father had obviously tried to scour off.

I ran my fingers over the taps, up the spout, poked them down into the drain hole, around the overflow trap, along the wall behind the tub, the crack where it met the tiles, the soap tray.

Not even a hair.

I looked around. The back seat of the car was empty.

"Dad, where is…?" I wanted to say *she*.

"Oh! Right. I put it downstairs."

I looked at him, puzzled. "You mean the basement?"

His mouth twitched, embarrassed.

I checked my watch and looked at the sky. The cemetery counsellor was expecting us there by three for the interment. It was about to pour and we had a twenty-minute drive ahead of us.

"Dad, where exactly?"

"In the freezer."

"What, next to the beef?"

He hesitated and then nodded.

In spite of myself I recoiled as I hit the light at the top of the stairs; her presence there—her oppress-ence—was still so strong. I had tried for years to pretend the basement wasn't part of our house, avoided going down there, kept the door shut, my ears shut against her whenever she was there, although this had been more difficult in winter when the furnace carried her voice up through the hot-air vents.

I put out a hand to keep from hitting the lintel as I

began to descend, afraid either I'd brain myself or the foundations would shift somehow and trap me—a nightmare I'd had since childhood, after reading of a child in Mexico, trapped by earthquake under plaster and beams, forced to gnaw off her own hand to get free. Mother, two inches shorter than me, was unbothered by the tight turns of the stairwell. If anything, its closeness comforted her. She liked to hide with her sickness in the laundry room, away from the rest of us, preferring the companionship of old lawn furniture, figure skates, snow boots and Christmas ornaments, her record player cranked up high, singing along with—and often, disconcertingly, against—the music she had loved.

At the bottom of the stairs, in the swinging shadows of our winter coats, I saw her loom, its wooden frame and crosspieces disassembled and roped together neatly by my father, like a grown-up's playpen. Beyond the furnace, stretching to the far end of the basement, were the shelves my father had put up to hold her preserves and mounted on the opposite wall, my canoe paddles, our snowshoes, an assortment of rusting tools and hardware, my father's framed degree.

I raised the lid of the freezer. Right beside the Tintoretto beef was a forest green cardboard box. I lifted it out, unable to resist thinking: *smaller than a breadbox, bigger than a mouse.*

I'd never seen human ashes before. I opened the lid

and undid the plastic bag inside. A puff of ash curled out and hung, twinkling, in the air. I stirred it with my finger and it vanished. There was an envelope with a slip of paper inside showing her full name, the date of the cremation and the cemetery's crest. I took out a handful of her ashes and spread it with my thumb, tilting my palm to the light. Fine gravel made of pulverized bone chips that were satiny like the lining of seashells flecked with colours, wine, blue, grey, pink, mixed with a sandy yellow dust that clung to my fingers. I touched my tongue to it and tasted—chalk. I poured what I held in my hand, about three teaspoons, into the envelope which I folded and put in my pocket, then I wiped my fingers on my shirt and carried the box out to the car.

It was the colour and size of my shoe sole. The animal smell assailed my nostrils as a thin stream of vapour rose up from my plate. The dark liquid seeping out of its pores stained a corner of my potatoes and I felt four years old again, wanting to slip it to the dog. I sawed off a piece, steadying the operation with my fork. A tough band of membrane, shiny and sleek as elastic, resisted my blade. I peeled the flesh free of it. From the freshly cut edge, blood welled brightly and my yellow beans drew it up like a sponge. I patted the piece on my fork against a dab of mustard, staining that with blood. I put my fork down again. I hadn't been back a week and already I felt ready to explode. Why couldn't my father accept who I was?

My father was watching with annoyance. "So that's it? Never again?"

I sighed. "I think not."

"I've got a whole side of Blue Ribbon Beef in the freezer. I'll never get through it alone."

"So give it away. There's lots of meat-eaters in this town.... Wait a minute. Blue Ribbon Beef?" My father's eyes shifted away from mine and all of a sudden I got it.

37

"Tintoretto slabbed you! You're working for them. I don't believe this."

"Frederika, let me explain."

"What's to explain? They're major polluters, head offices in Johannesburg!"

"That connection's been disproved."

"Oh, but it hasn't. You admitted that yourself before I left."

"Frederika, it's time you listened up."

"You mean sell out. No thanks."

"I thought that mountaintop of yours discouraged being judgemental."

"Dirty pool, Dad. We're discussing Tintoretto and the fact that their welcome-aboard cow is in your freezer."

"It's done. *Fait accompli.* I've already signed."

I pushed back my chair and stood up. "No point fighting."

"Funny, you've been angry with me ever since you got back. What's eating you, Frederika? You think I'm responsible for what happened, don't you? What is it you want from me?" A vein was standing out on his temple.

I hung my head. "I don't know."

We'd had such a pleasant talk earlier that day. I had told him about Yin and Yang, the Asian principle of opposites, how some foods, for instance, were female, some male, each reacting differently on the tongue. He had rummaged through the fridge, wanting to guess which vegetable was which, but he came up wrong as often as right. "Harder than sexing a kitten," he'd joked, spitting a sliver of ginger out into his palm. He recalled predicting I'd be a girl, although even in labour my mother was convinced she'd delivered a boy. You've made a mistake, Doctor, she had said. Look again. No mistake.

When I described the wheel of cause and effect and reincarnation, he dismissed the notion, thought the idea of an animal coming back as a human was ridiculous. How could anyone believe that.

"You find angels and devils more credible—"

"Christians today don't have to believe the Bible literally. Your people can prove reincarnation?"

I had smiled. "My people?"

~

The mist in the air was gradually giving way to a fine rain, stopping the light down to a dull ochre, barely enough to see by, although it was still early afternoon. I had meditated in my room most of the morning. Now I felt the urge to do physical work. I decided the outside of the house needed cheering up, so I drove out and bought gardening supplies, came back and dug up the beds below the verandah, dragged the two bags of loam and manure out of the back of the car, slit their ears and poured them in, black as soot against the original earth. I laid out flats of annuals at intervals along the bed and began arranging them by colour.

It had been years since I'd worked these beds, the summer after high school, and I craved the stickiness and odour of earth, the thoughts that accompanied planting. In weather like this the Nepalis would never have risked gardening; I was inviting vapours to enter my lungs—evil dampness settling into my upper warmer, triggering a hollow heat condition elsewhere. Slippery pulse, coated tongue. A predilection towards Yin deficiency.

A few inches below the surface of the flower bed the earth changed, no longer sticky, more granular. The refrigerated draught of winter rose into the palm of my hand although it was now well into April. A cardinal in the maple overhead sang through the rain for his mate, repeating his pattern without pause as if not wanting to give silence a chance to answer.

I turned the plastic germination pots over and nudged the seedlings out—cubist plugs of ivory root coil—cosmos, alyssum, portulaca, pansies, one glorious Icelandic poppy, forget-me-nots, hens-and-chicks for the rock border, an illicit wild trillium, petunias, impatiens, their names like cosmetics for snow queens: tangerine ice, coral blush, loganberry frost. Rain pattered down onto their pale petal ears. I straightened my back and surveyed the bed. My shoulders had already begun to sting no matter which way I twisted to stretch them but I wanted to get everything planted before nightfall.

My nails were black with grave dirt from the day before, my fingers jamming the wire wreath deep into the ground, blowing granite dust out of the freshly cut corners of her name.

Keep her down. What, still angry? The pansies looked crowded next to the alyssum. I pulled a clump out, tore their root ball in two and plugged them in on either side. Room to breathe. *While she remains absolutely breathless. . . . Keep her down and get on with it.* The cosmos will shade the impatiens. The poppy next to that. "Let's we forget," the private school wisecrack, whispered down the rows at assembly every November eleventh, circa tenth grade when the buds of acerbity burst into full flower. A perennially showy display, the tiny marker read, as were we in those days. *The best is behind me, the worst beneath me. Keep her down.* . . . The black bed was riddled with little burrows I'd trowelled out, their corresponding scoops of earth beside them, waiting to be filled. From the steps to the end of the house was one long snake of pinks, violets, apricots, whites. Baby pastels the only stock I could find this late into planting.

Every time I weeded, new stones appeared, potsherds, rusty keys, a scrap of leather, a plastic poker chip, the earth yielding up her dead, her toxic waste. I read in the sine wave of the cedar fence the places where the earth had tried to expel each probing post, contracting around the ones it was forced to accept.

Her birthstone, amethyst, her gravestone an obelisk of basalt, black and glittering, strong and decisive. Divisive. Tearing the clouds in two as they floated overhead, the day of the service.

The rain was getting thicker, no longer a dismissable Irish mist. It was running down my hood, sliding into my upturned cuffs, collecting in the furrows. The chill was penetrating my muscles, shirring up my lungs, a dull ache creeping down my spine into my kidneys. A muscle in my mind twitched and whatever I'd been thinking at that instant was swept away. My intent—had I been about to stick my trowel here or there? How long had my hand been poised above this hole? Was this how her disease began? I threw down my trowel and stood up. The blood pooled, sun discs spinning across my vision, fingers fizzing, eardrums roaring. I bent over to bring my head to heart level and waited. Reduced to this. Locked in a ridiculous bow to my half-finished handiwork, afraid to move for fear I'd pass out, knowing that my mind had folded a pleat of memory into time—not sure how deep the fold or whether what I'd lost would ever come back.

〜

Coming back from shopping I found myself turning down the top of what had once been Renie's street. Renie had been a kind of grandmother to me at a time when my own mother was too sick to notice me. She died the summer I graduated from high school.

I stood at the gate and looked again at Cawthra House, still standing empty, its brown brick spotted with the detached suckers of ivy that had reached the eaves, then gradually withered back to nothing. Its heavy windows, set like eyes above the front door, its sandstone sills, discoloured by years of accumulated soot and snow, ran streaks from their corners like dirty tears. The very name of the place sounded like a catch in the throat. Centred between the two windows was a third eye, circular, with leaded panes and a decorative slab below it that resembled a folded napkin. She used to fling that window open with a distracted smile like a character from a nursery rhyme, startling the squirrels into flight.

I had first been invited inside, with my friends, one Hallowe'en night. She admired our costumes, talked to us as though we were her equals although we were no older than ten or eleven. It was a new experience for me to be taken serously and as a teenager I began to visit her regularly, dropping in on my way home from school. Cawthra House was a respite from my family situation. Renie would help me with my homework and then we'd have a snack in front of the television, a pleasure forbidden back home, and we would talk. "What's happening with your mother these days, Frederika?"

"Absolutely no improvement. She's gone off food again and sleeps mostly, won't talk to anyone. I guess she's made up her mind to die." In the silence that had followed, I could sense Renie's own death approaching. She'd made a joke about that once: "Time flies," and swatted at the air around her head and laughed.

"How's your father handling it?"

"He doesn't say much either but I overheard him on the phone, arguing with her doctors that they had to readmit her. He's convinced the new medication's making her worse."

"It must be like caring for a child."

Mum, belted into her chair at the dining-room table, fooling with her pearls, pulling the long string against the lip of the table, bup-bup-bup, *bewitched by the sound, her food congealing. My father, mouth twitching throughout dinner, snatching out a hand, snapping the string, pearls bouncing into corners—*

"A little."

Renie would take my hand and I was able to leak a little of the shame and anger out, feeling relief in being able to talk about the person I could no longer talk to and then she would serve up bowls of her stewed chicken. Her kitchen was squalid, her failing eyes no longer capable of spotting the dirt. The ancient mosaic tiles on her counter were grouted with filth—in sharp contrast to the sanitary regimen a series of housekeepers was inflicting on me back home.

I was entering my fastidious phase at that time, guarding the portals of my body, scrubbing my hands to avoid contagion with my mother's disease the moment I left her room or after talking to my father if he'd been in contact with her. I washed my hands after they touched the banister, her tray, the faucets, the doorknobs, held my breath when I passed her room on the landing, let a minute pass before walking through air she had occupied.

The dirt-etched gentility of Cawthra House was hideous and fascinating with its perpetually drawn drapes, musty throws and dim passageways protected from light's scrutiny, but it was a safe house, carrying nothing of my mother's illness.

Renie carved open the boiled chicken on the bare tiles, scooping the soft flesh up with a spoon onto my plate. A little red sauce on the side, strings of celery, whole peppercorns rolling in the juice.

Across town, on Champagne Street, in the steamy windows of Chinese noodle houses, barbecued ducks hung from gummy hooks. It fascinated me that there was never any report of sickness. Something the Chinese did with spices maybe. Whenever the men from the health department checked they found nothing. The Chinese understood sickness long before microscopes. That November, a doctor in Toronto gave a lecture explaining how he successfully resurrected bacteria scraped from the viscera of Egyptian mummies.

And grant us all eternal life . . .

One evening, I had rolled up my sleeves and begun washing our dishes, thinking Renie was upstairs on the phone when she appeared without warning at my side. Her rheumy old eyes widened at the sight of my freshly scarred wrist and she seized both my hands in hers with a look of immense tenderness crossed with such great anger that it frightened me. "It's okay, Renie." I pulled back, concerned for her heart but she only gripped me tighter.

"It is not okay. You've done this to someone I love."

That night marked the beginning of our real intimacy. I could tell her the worst and she always lifted off half my burden. Time and again she put a halo of possibility around conditions that for me had seemed unalterable. Renie tried to show me how to live by her rules, without loneliness or regrets, to be confident of my power rather than to live in dread of what the next moment might bring. Renie refused to retreat from anything, neither her bad heart nor the tough conversation. We had talked about completion. She was ready.

One summer morning, she was found in her garden, sitting in a chair, still looking up into the trees. The ambulance pulled up quietly outside Cawthra House and the attendants stepped down without haste, opening the double doors at the back, sliding out the stretcher. The neighbour who'd telephoned them stood on the sidewalk waiting to usher them through the house to the back. I sat down on the lawn opposite and nodded distantly to her, afraid I'd be called upon to help. I couldn't handle seeing Renie that way.

The ambulance men came out, the contours of her body recognizable beneath the bright orange blanket. They slid the stretcher in. Renie's neighbour locked the front door of the house and they drove off together.

The beating of death's wings in my ears.

Renie never locked her back door. We're in Port Airedale, darling, she used to drawl. I tiptoed past the gardening tools and rubber boots in the back porch, opened the screen door and stepped into the kitchen. Remarkably, the odour of Renie's soup lingered although it must have been days since she'd last cooked. Dishes were stacked everywhere and a sour smell hovered about the fridge. The grandfather clock in the hall whose phases of the moon visibly shifted with the clicking of tiny cogs suddenly erupted at the quarter hour with a chime that made my heart jump.

For the first time I was alone in Renie's bedroom. Her

bedclothes had been twisted into a rope and thrown aside. Tucked into the mirror of her dressing table were photos of her husband, long gone, and a new one that I recognised with a start was of Renie as a baby, a wriggling blur in a high chair. On either side of the mirror were clutches of make-up pots, hairpin trays, brooches, earrings, astringent bottles looking ancient, funerary, as though gathered to accompany her soul to the afterlife.

I didn't dare go into her bathroom, afraid I might find a piece of flesh, a bloody cloth, footprint of death itself, despite knowing she'd died peacefully among her flowers, as she had wished. I closed the bedroom door behind me and then remembered I'd found it open and pushed it ajar again, anxious to leave things as I'd found them. I felt her presence, hovering.

Time flies.

Suddenly, the full realization of Renie's flight, her empty room, window flung ajar, all further conversations between us—yet no tears came and I stopped feeling anything at all for some time after that.

Today, remembering her, I leaned against her front gate and was able to cry for her at last.

My father was not an extravagant present-giver. He and I knew the tomato red canvas canoe with two cedar paddles the colour of honey was compensation for my mother's illness and my being sent away to boarding school that year. The canoe was a pleasure that money could buy.

My father and I strapped it to the top of the car and drove north for an hour to a quiet stretch of the Hart River for my first solo voyage, gentle water that wound its way down into Port Airedale, eventually emptying into the Sound.

We parked and he carried the canoe himself down the steep bank, set it in the water, and when I had climbed in he passed over the paddle with ceremony and pushed me off, his face radiant as a boy's. We arranged to rendezvous at four.

The river was about thirty feet wide, shallow and slow moving with regular bends, perfect beginner's water. I let the canoe drift towards the middle of the stream, feeling the sensation of the current as it turned the bow downstream. The riverbank foliage looked tropical with midsummer spears of lupines, cardinal flowers, jewelweed, Veronica, columbine, willows trailing their fingers, ferns looking crosshatched at a distance. Both banks were identical and the water a dark reflection of the sky, so that the effect was of floating through mirrors. Even my body felt split symmetrically, one set of muscles pulling against their opposite as I paddled.

The river was the temperature of blood and my fingers felt no sensation touching it. I wanted to slip over the side and enter it like a dream, swim for hours without effort or drift down its grey-green waters until nightfall, in a prehistoric world, leather-winged pterodactyls circling overhead, plated reptilia nosing through the sun-soaked mud of the banks beyond.

The ripples left by my strokes, the ferns, the overhanging branches, the absolute stillness of siesta hour, the canoe, sibilant through reeds, the humid air clinging like skin, the kindly, domestic water, brackish with iron that dyed my fingers to the knuckle and swallowed the paddle when I thrust it to sound the bottom.... A moment of perfect happiness.

It was hard not to subject happiness to analysis, that I might learn to control it somewhat, possess it, conjure it up at will. But studying such moments meant stuffing them into the killing jar. I paddled along, setting myself adrift in sensations without words—eye-thought, ear-thought, nose-thought. A flash of blue kingfisher broke through a bar of sunlight and vanished. A frog, markings lucid in the shadow of the canoe, clung to a stump, its outstretched legs undulating in the swirl of vegetable curds my stroke had disturbed. When the water cleared he was gone.

A willow stood at the curve of the next bank and I decided to tie up to it and go ashore for a bit. The bow of the canoe parted the curtain of branches and bunted into soft mud. I stepped out, finished my knot and was thinking again how peaceful everything was when the air shifted, carrying something back in its jaws—only a whiff but it was unmistakable—and then the wind wheeled again and fetched back plain mud and crushed ferns and I thought I'd only imagined the other. I sat down to buckle on my sandals when I heard a ticking buzz coming from a clump of tall grass to my right, as though bees were mating with grasshoppers. I got up and cocked my ear, trying to identify it, and that's when I caught the smell again. Choking. Beyond fecal or vegetable, definitely the blunt stink of carrion. My stomach flexed, coming to its separate recognition. The ticking and the smell were together, somehow. Tentatively I began probing the clump of grass beside me with my paddle.

I walked around it and was investigating the far side when my blade encountered a firmness—fleshy, not rock or dirt. The ticking crescendoed. I folded back the grass with my blade and saw a boiling sack of rice, a scrap of fur with ringtail markings, the rib cage swarming with beetles brilliant as fish lures, shuttling in and out of the cavity of what had once been a raccoon.

I withdrew my paddle and the grasses sprang shut.

I never told my father. He would have ridiculed my squeamishness about what was, after all, a natural phenomenon but, more particularly, in those days we believed our family's survival depended upon concealing unpleasantness from one another, whether physical or emotional. We sacrificed whatever comfort we might have received in order to spare one another further turbulence, thus imagining we were exercising a measure of damage control, but at a cost. We privately acquired a vast suspicion of happiness—a façade, after all—and our fears were confirmed. It was riddled through from behind, maggoty: my mother's smile widening to reveal yellowed teeth, drug-darkened gums; her buoyant weeks inevitably presaging those of sepia; my father's plaster joviality over breakfast after a night spent rocking her, gibbering and hysterical, in his arms behind a closed door down the hall.

Exposing the filth between the tiles.

⌒

She came in to say goodnight, her silks crumpling into a
rose around her as she sat down on the bed. She inclined
her face to mine and an earring slid, chilly, across my
cheek.

She straightened up, pulling the heavy strands of
pearls from between her breasts. I caught a length, warm
from her skin, and let it slide through my fingers, then
took my mother's left hand and spread her fingers to
examine them. A diamond engagement ring with emer-
alds, plain wedding band next to it. On her other hand,
sapphires. Next to it a fire opal from my grandmother's
estate and a violet-coloured stone. I breathed on it.

"Amethysts keep you sober, according to the Greeks.
I'll find out tonight." Her eyes sparkled with mischief. "I
love good champagne."

I tilted her hand this way and that, squinting to make
the sapphires bleed into spindles through my eyelashes. "I
don't think that's such a good idea."

"You promised not to worry. Remember?" She bent
down and kissed me again. "Go to sleep. Someday this
jewellery will be yours and you'll be going to a fancy-dress
ball yourself." A rustle as she stood up. "Light off?"

I nodded. "Mum?"

She stood waiting in silhouette at the door.

"Can you be happy?"

She laughed and swept out of the room without answering, leaving a trace of perfume on my pillow that lingered there until morning.

Sighs. Whisperings down the hall. From my parents'
room. My mother cried out sharply—not in pain, exactly.
They were *doing* it!

Caught between wanting to get out of bed or burrow
down out of earshot, I did both—burrowed down, ears
cocked.

A thump. Heavy. I felt it through my bedframe. *Thump*
again. My mother crying out, more in anger this time.
And something else. Unrecognizable. Make it again. *No,
don't.*

I lifted my head clear of the pillow. Low rumble of
both voices. A fight?

I couldn't stand it. I got up, pulled the bedspread
around me, went to my door and peered over the banister.
Bright light on the floor below, leaked out from under my
parents' door. My mother was making little noises, rhymi-
cally—like a cat, mewling. So this was sex?

Crash! An explosion of light. My father's shout of sur-
prise. Murmurs for a moment, then his voice raised:
"Frederika?"

I tried to sound startled. "Dad?" Heart pounding.
Not going down there.

"Are you awake?" His voice tight.

I dropped my bedspread, went to the top of the stairs. "Yes."

"Call an ambulance. The number's by the kitchen phone."

I went to their door. "Is Mum okay?" Let there be no blood. Nothing to clean up.

"She's fine. Just go make that call."

I took the stairs two at a time, found the number and began dialling, pulling the phone to the floor in my haste so that I was forced to kneel under the table as I gave directions, pleading with the dispatcher to hurry.

I pulled my father's bush jacket off its hook and threw it on over my nightclothes, then went outside onto the verandah to watch for the ambulance. I could hear my mother's moans upstairs, regular, rhythmic, so sexual it made the hairs prickle on my arms.

The ambulance pulled into the drive, lights flashing, and two attendants jumped down and pulled out a stretcher, bright red blanket, straps and buckles. *Buckles!* Across the street a neighbour pulled back her curtain.

"Second floor. First room on your right." I pointed inside with a long finger. In the belfry.

I watched their feet climbing past the spindles. White centipede wriggling up the staircase. Outside, the stars and moon were pale against the glow of the ambulance lights, the high-tech, metallic interior of the van. I tucked my hands, Chinese style, up the cuffs of the coat, wrapping my fingers around each elbow to warm them. I couldn't stop sniffing the sleeves, savouring the boaty odour of oiled canvas and mildew, happier days.

Commotion on the landing.

I drew back into the shadows to hide, then thought better of it and stepped out again. The two attendants were struggling with the stretcher on the stairs, my mother's back arching in convulsions, my father pressing her down by the shoulders, Mother's chin upthrust, eyes rolling white in their sockets, turning to look directly at me now—oh God, Mum, don't. Froth sliding down her cheek like detergent down a glass. Hands, two birds flapping under the belts.

Let this cup pass from me.

I am far, far, away. Watching the stretcher come out. Watching what is inside my mother and me come out.

This time, when I found her, she had wandered outside, down to the bottom of the garden. She was staring into the clouds, making a flutey glissando cry into a trumpet of her hands that made my scalp prickle. She paused, then made her cry again, hooting into an empty sky.

She had been home from the hospital less than a month.

"Mum"—I touched her shoulder, careful not to startle—"everything okay?"

She shushed me, finger across her lips, pointing up into the firs.

I saw nothing.

"You hear that?"

I shook my head, scared now, turning to run into the house and telephone my father.

She seized my arm. "Silly goose. Look!" She pointed again. Through the top branches, close to the trunk, I could make out a black shape, a glint of eye. The raven's beak opened and out came the sound she'd been trying to imitate—of water being poured up a flute.

She turned and threw me a look of pure triumph, shook my arm so hard I staggered, giggling out my relief,

"Yes, yes. I see it now. I do."

After the doctor had left and my mother was beginning to drift off to sleep, I crept into her room and straightened her covers, poured fresh ice water into her glass. She opened her eyes and reached for my hand. "Oh, hon, my feet. Would you mind?"

Her heels were icy. The sedative always seemed to restrict her circulation. I rubbed some warmth back into them, put on woollen socks and tucked her feet back under the covers. There was a dreamy smile on her face now, although her eyes were closed, her hands folded across her breast as though in death. I lifted them to her sides.

"You're such a help, Frederika, like a little mother to me."

Suddenly it rang.

We both reached for the phone but my father got there first.

"For whom?" His puzzlement vast. "She's not here. Who's calling? Yes, of course I'll accept. Isabel? Isabel, is that you? Where in—Isabel? Hello, Operator?"

Shaken, he replaced the receiver and stared at me. "Sounded like a highway behind her. She was calling, person to person, asking for *herself*."

I pushed open the vestibule door. "Mum, I'm home." She was on the phone, her laughter coming from the kitchen. "Emily and Martina are here too. Anything to eat?" No answer. My girlfriends followed in single file after me. "Mum?"

She was still laughing and carrying on. Flitting shadow across my heart. "Mum?" I led my friends into the kitchen.

She was all alone, standing at the window, talking a blue streak, except that the phone was sitting on the table across the room. I turned around to block my girlfriends' view, pushed them back out into the hall before they could catch a glimpse, figure out my mother had gotten off between floors, was a few bricks shy of a load, not exactly wound too tight.

"My mother's busy making dinner right now. Let's go into the garden. She'll come out and visit when she's finished."

Lights on. Nobody home.

"Slut. Alleycat! You little minx!" she hissed at me from the top of the stairs as I came in the door, her face contorted, one hand hiding something behind her back.

My library books slid to the floor with a bang. "Mum, what are you talking about?"

"Filthy. You. Ugh. There." She made as if to spit over the railing at me and as she straightened, I saw what it was she was hiding from me.

My face coloured as I began climbing towards her, my hand outstretched, choking back my rage. "Give it to me, Mum. It's mine. You had no right to look at that." I kept my voice steady in spite of the hot shame on my cheeks at the thought of what she had read. I dared not risk an escalation—the word my father and I used—when her mouth and eyes looked like that. When she was agitated anything could happen—and Dad was sure to hold me responsible for this one.

I climbed another stair. If she gave my diary right back I would love her forever and someday even forgive her, but instead she retreated one maddening step beyond reach, holding it over her head, her mouth working to get out the words.

"Shop-soiled goods! Wait until your father hears. Get away from me. Away!"

She meant it, shooing me with an authoritative, repelling hand the way she had a skunk once, at a picnic.

Renie was in Florida until New Year's. The boy I'd written about was away skiing with his family. My girl-friends were sick of hearing about my mother. I was all alone, and this time, I thought, I can't bear it.

I had to. Nothing to be done. I turned and went back downstairs, the muscles in my arms tight with wanting to grab her, throw her over the banister, rip my diary away from her, belt her, make her bleed. Her and her fucking Andrews Sisters.

I went into the kitchen, picked up the phone and pleaded a message into my father's machine to come home early, pulled three steaks from the freezer and threw them into the sink. She certainly wouldn't be well enough to do any cooking tonight.

It was dark. Still no sign of my father. Then I remembered: he'd gone off to Belleville to visit a client. He wouldn't be home until after eleven. Mum had retreated into the laundry room in the basement to play her records, shouting abuse over them at me whenever I opened the door and tried to coax her to eat, so I gave up and put her tray at the top of the stairs as though she were a wild animal I was trying to befriend. Miraculously, over the relentless *choo-choo* harmonics of her harpies, I heard the rattle of cutlery as she carried the tray back to her lair and felt a surge of relief that she was cooperating to some extent, together with something else so fierce and unspeakable that I began to choke and knew that if I didn't get out of the house that very instant I would die or go crazy too. I threw on my coat and boots and slammed the front door loud enough for the dead to hear.

Stars.

Snow, deep blue by moonlight. The rattle of a train, almost twenty miles away. Crackle of air hitting my lungs.

It was so cold in the garage that I knew I would feel next to nothing. I pulled my socks off, tucked them into my boots and squatted, flexing my toes by the light of my flash until I had located a spot on the instep between the bones and the tendons. I pushed the tip of the ice pick in. Slight tingling. I closed my eyes and pushed harder, and when I pulled it out again a red ball came up and burst into a web that trickled warmth down into the furrow between each toe. Then I did the other foot.

The snow felt soft and feathery underfoot as I stepped outside. By the time I reached the house the bleeding had stopped and my tracks were clear, no trace left of anything that could lead to questions being asked later. I stood on the porch and looked down at what I'd done, my wounds as beautiful and classic as any I'd seen in paintings.

~

Floating, flying, spying at night. Springing onto my neighbour's sill, catlike, from the bushes below, drawn to the yellow light, the family, replete, rising from the dining-room table to regroup around the hearth fire, every hair illuminated, making room on the couch, laughter, easy intimacy, one hand brushing the newel post as mother climbs to check on the baby, the other cupping her daughter's head beside her, arms about waists as they descend, kisses exchanged, curling up under the afghan to read their picture book together, the boy poking the fire, father's eyes unfurling in contented thought. The log pops and a maternal hand darts out to reassure.

Sleepwalkers, dreamy-eyed, torn from the frontispiece of a children's novel.

Hate it.

Burn them up.

Pressing my face against the cold window, drawing familial warmth like a thief through the glass into my veins before swimming off the sill to ride the darkness to the next house.

Invisible, as always, on my solitary night rounds.

This was the pattern.

Whenever things got bad at home, sooner or later, I dreamed about horses, night mares—like the one that shrank to the size of a dog when I tried to mount it, darting out from under the saddle skirt, snatching at the blanket with needle teeth. The soft horse whose jaws stretched like taffy, tearing through at the hinges from the pressure of the bit, cobalt sky through the eyeholes. The cadaverous one that scrambled upright onto two tottery legs, sucking in its breath until the saddle slid down around its fetlocks. The party horse I couldn't shake free of, whinnying inanities at my elbow down an endless corridor. The painted coquette, flirting under its eye-lashes, snatching at my lasso with its teeth, outrageous, unrepentant.

But on good nights, one horse recurred, a chess knight with chiselled curls and eyes like my father's, who stepped out of my dream to offer advice and insight, although his thinking was somewhat linear at times. He was a herd animal, after all, preferring to follow, nose to tail, his vision divided by bony muzzle.

When I awoke it wasn't to recall the specific details of

our conversation, just to savour the comforting residue his presence left behind.

The horses sacrificed their wisdom for me, suppressed instinct, allowing themselves to be caught as I waded in among them and, on good nights, letting me climb aboard, direct them this way and that with a squeeze. They were captive listeners, indulgent, equanimitous as I talked to them, in a language that helped nocturnally to order and make sense of my days.

Happiness is a Barb. Above the words, a white Arabian stallion with henna-dyed mane and kohl-lined eyes as beautiful as a woman's, reared against the pyramids of Giza. I pinned the poster to the wall opposite my bed, dreaming up names I would call a horse like this of my own. Now that I was taking lessons at the Airedale Equestrian Club, I wheedled my father to consider the idea of buying me a horse but every time I brought it up he refused. Horses terrified him, those huge bodies governed by brains no bigger than a peach—too much like dinosaurs, he said. As for horsey people, he thought they looked a lot like horses.

I was afraid of horses too but it was exhilarating to feel in possession of such power and speed and beauty. I found horses far more predictable than people. They were a mystery that could be explained.

My instructor told my father I had potential.

You and your mother, he said. Manipulators, both of you. You put your instructor up to that. But I was allowed to continue with my lessons.

The year my mother became too sick to function and had to be hospitalized I was sent to boarding school in Toronto and my riding lessons stopped, but I cut classes and ran away to all three horse shows—the Royal Winter Fair, Quarterama and the Arabian—watching just outside the show-ring gates where the riders lined up, waiting for their numbers to be called. Between events I slipped backstage to the stalls, strolling past security with rolled-up programme in hand—the heavy, five-dollar one professionals carried, with breeder indexes and stud genealogy charts that made Latin declensions read like Dick and Jane. The banners, tack chests and folding chairs, set up outside the stalls, were imprinted with the name of each farm and its stud, along with displays of fees, pedigrees, stable facilities, ribbons, trophies and framed photos of their champions, spread-eagled in show pose, ears flicked forward, neck arched, eyes red in the flash. Some owners played continuous videotapes showing the "floating action" of their "real movers" cantering endlessly into the camera.

I patted the horses through the bars of their stalls, deliberately impregnating my blazer cuffs with the smell I would savour, like a lover, for days afterwards. Without a horse of my own I lacked equine credentials. The horsey world would have nothing to do with me as I strolled down the aisles of box stalls, some fixed up for humans to sleep in, with curtains and camp cots, racks of ribbons, saddle blankets, buggy whips, the ubiquitous coffee thermos—bedroom interiors as mystical and romantic as the tents of Bedouin nomads.

Eventing was my secret passion. Cross-country endurance riding up cliffs, across rivers, not the showy, formal disciplines of dressage or jumping. I wanted to be adopted by a ranching family, throw my stuff into the back of a trailer airbrushed with bucking broncos, inherit a new life, foster parents—pragmatic, laconic, sane people who'd give me a colt to train under tireless personal supervision, with unstinting encouragement.

I would shuck my name, change it to Kim or Alex, braid my hair, get windburned freckled cheeks, strong wrists.

The girls at school ridiculed me, neighed and pawed the ground when I approached, but I didn't care. The sweet intoxicants of harness leather, horses and bedding, even of manure, brought on a kind of fever in me, a flush of adrenalin like spotting a movie star on the street. The slurry of shod hooves over cobblestones flooded me with sharp nostalgia for a horsedrawn past I'd never actually known—for a simpler life on the Channel Islands of Guernsey, Jersey and Sark, where cars were banned. The buggy culture of the Amish strongly attracted me but I did have reservations about the dress code. My mother's experiments in fashion, pressed on me as though I were her doll, had made me wary of unusual clothing.

My fellow equestriennes ... Beyond our shared obsession, I had nothing in common with the girls from the Equestrian Club. I had to accept it. I'd rarely ridden the same school horse twice while these girls had actually assisted at the births of their own animals, had broke and trained them by hand, their tack room walls fluttering with more ribbons than their prom gowns. I learned to drive a car instead, the standard shift allowing me mastery over another kind of horsepower. Eventually, dreaming about horses became something I did only occasionally and always at night.

I nudged my door shut carefully so as not to attract her attention again and flung myself back down on my bed to study for my history final. From downstairs came the insect whirr of her spinning wheel, the *crik-crik* of her foot on the treadle, her *Songs from the Hebrides* record, music quite conducive to study were it not that she kept snatching off the phonograph needle in mid-song, dropping it onto the next, listening for a few bars, then snatching it off again, searching for a song she seemed never to find.

In the space of days, gripped by her latest obsession, Mother had taken over the ground floor, woven us all into her spider's nest of raw wool, ripe with tallow and manure. She wound long warp yarns around an arrangement of dining-room chairs that effectively blocked our comings and goings, sorted skeins and stacked them, waist-high, in corners, then abandoned them forever. Cauldrons of dye simmered day and night on the kitchen stove—vile-smelling liquors of onion skin and goldenrod, madder and woad, mordanted with cream of tartar. Freshly dyed skeins, suspended over the sink from a broom handle, dripped a technicolour wound down the plaster, across the marble countertop to the floor.

We lived mostly now on take-out food and cold cereal, eaten, as we squatted, sans chairs and table, against the walls of the dining room.

Mother's research led her to conclude that she should buy a live Merino-Leicester crossbred sheep and keep it tethered in the backyard, wrapped in a canvas coat to ward off brambles and rainwater which stained fleece. My father, plunging into counter-research, located a source of perfectly acceptable Merino fleece on a farm near Madoc, Ontario, only a few hours' drive away, and she surrendered her breeders' catalogues without a struggle. The loom she ordered came shipped in pieces all the way from Salem, Massachusetts, and took us the better part of three days to assemble. The living room was big enough to accommodate it after we took out the couch and the hi-fi.

The first fruits of the loom were sleeveless vests in beige worsted intended for my father and me. Medieval-looking and itchy, they reached almost to the knee and were oily enough to be waterproof. In spite of the April warmth she insisted I wear mine to school. Up until now, my friends, typically appearance-conscious young women, had shown tolerance for my home situation; it made them grateful to have normal mothers of their own whose demands were moderate by comparison. But my arrival that morning dressed like one of Robin's Merry Men drew audible intakes of breath. I ate lunch by myself. I walked home alone. Torn between social ostracization and offence to my mother, I stashed the vest under a bridge on my way to school next morning, and picked it up again on my way home.

Final exams. I closed my eyes and recited once again the fragile alliances of Europe in the 1800s, the pivotal intrigues, the good and bad harvests.

The players:

Metternich:
  — and attitude of
  — and importance of in relation to
  — the Holy Alliance
  — European unity
  — the Hapsburg empire

Done.

Bismarck, Otto Edward Leopold von,
(Count, later Prince):
  — and revolutions of 1848, 1886
  — and role in defeat of Prussian liberalism
  — and architecture of Triple Alliance
  — and intellectual propensities of

Done.

The exam was worth seventy-five per cent of my final mark. I was sure to graduate with honours if I did well tomorrow. Which would secure my chances of—I hardly dared think it—getting into residence at University of Toronto the following autumn—

Smash of glass.

I opened my eyes. She must have pulled too hard, toppled one of the chairs into a window. I closed my eyes and went on: the Weimar Republic—

"Frederika? Need you. Just for a minute."

I slammed my books shut and rolled off the bed to my feet for the third time that afternoon. Wisps of staple hung suspended in the air downstairs, swirled like spindrift on the dining-room table, clotted the bookcases. We were constantly blowing them out our noses, grooming one another's clothing in passing like mandrills.

She was on her knees picking out daggers of glass from a pile of freshly carded fleece on the floor. Her fingers were bloody. I led her into the bathroom, bandaged her up, picked the fleece clean of glass, helped her rewind the skeins and went back upstairs. It was now almost four o'clock and I still had some eighty pages of textbook to review.

Songs from the Hebrides came floating upstairs. I rolled up a towel and wedged it under my door, which helped somewhat.

I finished studying sometime around one that morning but Mother had a bad night and didn't sleep at all, which meant I didn't either because she rattled away at her loom, paced the floor, muttered and called out to me or my father, singing our names at times, making up little rhymes with them. At dawn, groggy but still capable of rereading my notes, I slipped into my clothes to study but she heard me and called out.

I pulled my hair until my eyes watered. When my head was clear again, I went down.

She stood at the foot of the stairs holding up yards of dirty grey homespun, thick and coarse as an army blanket. Her night's labour. "For today," she smiled brightly. "Because I know it's special."

So she had noticed.

"Here, let me." Buckling a wide belt of my father's around my waist, she bustled around me like a couturier, tucking in generous pleats of homespun until I was swathed in a fat, prickly kilt that reached mid-calf. She flipped the trailing end over my left shoulder and drew it under the belt again at the back, then held me at arms' length to survey her handiwork. "I love it," she breathed with delight. "See? This is the original shepherd's check. Before tartans came along."

It could not, by any stretch, have been called a check and no self-respecting shepherd in the last five hundred years would have been caught dead in such a get-up.

I opened my mouth to snap at her, my eyes gritty with

fatigue and my stomach so tight I could scarcely draw breath, but her face was suffused with such a glow of self-congratulation that I made only a weak smile instead and stood there, suppressing the words that might have triggered another crash into her sepia state. She had been known to take to her bed on the ocean floor after such a scene, refusing to eat, to speak, to respond to light for weeks on end.

The Swing Era I called it, our lives together.

My father laughed out loud as he passed me on the stairs, then covered it with a cough.

Mother:
    — and her effect on others
    — and similarities to
    — and differences from
    — and fragile alliances with

I went into the bathroom, closed the door, took one long look in the mirror and turned the bathtub taps on full before allowing myself the luxury of an earsplitting howl through clenched jaws.

My father had promised to take me to dinner downtown in celebration of my driver's licence—just the two of us because it was Swing Era time again and Mother refused to come. She was holed up in her room, taking all her meals in bed like Titania, with her hair spread out on the pillow and make-up on and a silk jacket, while my father and I waited on her like a pair of besotted Bottoms. I hadn't seen her on her feet in over three weeks.

She had taken a particular dislike to me, this time around. When I showed her my licence in its little plastic slipcase she looked right past me to my father to complain about her tea.

We came into her room to leave her the phone number of the restaurant. My father leaned over to kiss her goodbye and that's when it started. She seized him by the necktie and tugged him close and pushed her tongue into his mouth. He was astonished at first and then he liked it. I stood there watching while they ate each other's face, making little kittenish noises, whispering sexy talk as though they'd completely forgotten I was there. She was such a hypocrite, using words more explicit than any I'd written in my diary. My father was sitting down on the bed now with his legs crossed and I could see why. My face flamed up and I thought I would suffocate.

I went and stood out in the hall, reminding him that our reservation was for six and it was almost that now. My mother broke off kissing and stared at me with little jealous eyes.

"You're not going anywhere with her." She pointed and began slinging filthy names at me, accusing me of stealing him, of performing sexual acts with him. He tried a bit to shush her up but he wasn't shocked or angry and never once defended me, only shrugging as if to say, nothing works when she's in this mood. He was actually enjoying her little performance and suddenly I despised them both and began shouting at him to make her shut up, goddamn it, she was the pig not me, but she just laughed and waved me away with her queenly hand and when I asked him again about dinner he handed over his wallet, told me to order whatever I wanted and to take the car, and then he got up and closed the bedroom door in my face.

So I took the car. I ordered steak and dessert and I left a big tip, then I drove past our house out to the highway and I pulled off at a trail I knew, safe and secluded, very beautiful, trees all around, and I opened the trunk and got the hammer and a two-inch nail out of the tool chest and by the light of the headlights kneeled on the bare rock and thought about the direction my life was taking until I felt the anger climb straight up my spine and I laid my hand against the rock, palm up, steadied the nail there with my middle fingers and brought the hammer down.

I'd meant to manage it alone but the cloth I'd brought soaked through in no time; I must have hit an artery. I hoped I wouldn't faint at the wheel. I was getting blood all over the seat but it couldn't be helped. At the hospital, I told them I'd torn my hand on a fence but they wanted to inform my parents. I insisted they were both too ill to be disturbed, but when I got up off the bed my father and the doctor who'd sewed me up were talking in the hall and I knew by their faces that neither of them had bought a word of my story.

In a way, it was a relief to be forced to talk. But it was short-lived because less than a week later my mother turned worse, leaving little notes around the house when we were asleep, accusing me of poisoning her, my father of having other women. She became violent, throwing trays, biting. She saved up her medication and overdosed one night, almost dying before we could get to her. My father was a wreck.

I thought I could handle it. I was getting out of there in the fall. I had won my scholarship to university in Toronto. Then in August she overheard certain of our plans and threatened to kill herself if we hospitalized her again and my father who was desperate begged me to stay at home just one more year and help him with this crisis.

By late October the worst had passed and she had begun to eat and dress herself again but it was too late for me to register for classes. The letter, informing me my space was no longer being held, was part of it, perhaps. Renie's death at the end of August had been another terrible blow, but there was no particular reason for me to have chosen the night that I did, save finding the sewing shears in the front hall, back from the sharpener, and being alone, my father having taken my mother to a movie.

I thought I'd learned something from the last time but, once again, the desire for release seized hold and refused to let go. I had to complete things.

I did it in my bedroom. Pinched up a fold of loose skin on my left side below my breast and snipped through and the hot spurt felt so bloody marvellous I couldn't stop. I pinched another handful below that and snipped again, then one more below that, the third cut extending below my waistband, blood and fluid running out. The pain was manageable but it swirled up and almost choked me every time I inhaled, so I sat down and found that by keeping my breaths shallow I could float just above it— except, again, I'd miscalculated the amount of bleeding and had to lie down on the floor with the towel balled up underneath my side to stop it but even that after a while ... There was a smell of rust as the warmth spread out under my shoulders like angel's wings.

Faint voices, beams of light, a door sliding beneath me. Trembling movement. White dwarfs down a corridor.

Later, a lawn chair. Birdsong. Sessions of therapy. Tentative recognitions. Discharged at last, to ride the long train home.

The following spring, I ran away to the East.

My father and I had drunk our way through all the bereavement liquor left in the house. He announced he was switching to beer, but these days I wanted a bottle of something hard to get me through the long evenings alone with him in the house.

I slipped out of the house early, finished my errands and was sitting on the steps of the liquor store, waiting for it to open and watching a flock of purple martins swoop for breakfast, when a young woman arrived and unlocked the door.

Her hair was odd, slicked back into a long ducktail and wet looking, and the way her eyes darted around when her head came up—a cormorant surfacing with its catch.

She waved me in. "Been waiting long?"

"Shaking and quaking since dawn."

"Funny, you don't look like an alkie. Not with those bags of"—she squinted to read the labels—"turtle beans, cracked wheat, tofu. Whew. Serious bran person here."

"I'm looking for vodka. Have you got Stolichnaya?"

She pointed to the list. "Rocket-fuel section."

I liked her flippancy, exotic as her haircut in a town

like Port Airedale. A pink triangle pin peeped out from under her lapel. Under it were the words: Silence = Death. She caught me reading it.

"Sheesh. And you a girl. You've never seen the pink triangle?"

"I know about the pink triangle."

"Good. The rest you can interpret variously, depending on your orientation." She squinted at me. "Speaking of pink triangles, any kind of a women's scene going on around here?"

I pondered that for a moment. "Do you curl?"

"Oh yeah. I'm very intense about my sweeping. Seriously."

"If you want a women's scene, I think you'll have to make your own."

Her face sagged. "Nothing in this town ever changes. I can hardly wait to get back."

"To?"

"McGill. *A Montréal.* I'm here visiting my granny for the summer."

"And your major?"

"Historiography."

I blinked. "What year?"

"Fifth. I'm doing it on the instalment plan." She plucked the order slip from my hand and vanished into the stacks.

"Smirnoff if there's no Stolie," I called after her.

"What exactly is historiography?"

She returned with a bottle in each hand. "The history of history. You know, men dipping their wicks in ink. I'm raising shit with my professors but I'm so good they're forced to give me the marks. Here's your Stolie." She banged the other bottle down beside it. "Ever tried this? It's Chinese. A vodka high at half the price but you absolutely have to drink it frozen. The bouquet is *formidable*." She pronounced it Parisian style, kissing her fingertips so earnestly and throwing them skyward that I laughed out loud and then stopped. Something about that gesture was familiar.

I squinted at the label. "Black Puppy? You've tried this?"

"Trust me." She laid the bottle down and rolled it up in a sheet of brown paper with the deftness of a cigar maker. "Say, do you ever hear of parties? I'm famished for some girlie action—oh, don't give me that look. I'm talking about talking. I find women broaden one, don't you?" She fluttered her lashes suggestively. "Let me introduce myself, although, actually, you know me—Lucille Flamand. Call me Luce."

"Not Monique's little sister!" That gesture. Of course.

"You and Monique were pretty tight back in eighty-one, weren't you?"

Equestrian Club daze. Falling under Monique's spell

had brought out the worst in me, played into my weakness for wanting to be liked by people like her at all costs, concealing my own personality in order to merge with hers. She was a temperamental person, hypercritical, imperious, a perfectionist. Her family eventually upped stakes and went back to Montreal but it took me months afterwards to purge myself of Monique's influence. Luce had been a little squirt of a tomboy, begging to tag along with us although she hated horses and thought the club was full of snobs.

"I idolized you back then. Of course, you were too busy helping Monique pull my wings off."

"Sorry." I felt awkward, my arms full of groceries, unable to make more than a shrug of contrition.

"Don't be. Humiliation builds character. Your folks still live in that haunted house up on Belvedere?"

"My dad does. My mum died this spring. I'm back here for a bit until things normalize."

"Funny word, that. Say, where've you been, in the army or something?" She pointed to my head.

"Hardly," I laughed. "A temple in Nepal."

"I was close. You celibate, a vegetarian, doing the holy thing?"

I smiled. "How is Monique, anyway?"

"Married to a lawn-products salesman with a kid and a half. He treats me like guano, Monique and the kids like chattels, and yet Monique had the gall last Christmas to suggest I seek professional help for my self-destructive sexual orientation. What about hers, I say. Anyway, enough about my family. Let's talk about you."

I put my bags down on the counter.

"Historiography sounds interesting. Tell me more about that."

The door opened and three customers walked in.

She offered to drop by my house around eight. Before parting, she seized my hand and twisted it into a three-part, hi-five soul handshake of farewell that I tried in vain to figure out all the way back to the car.

At eight-ten, the doorbell rang.

"We alone?" Luce whispered, her eyes darting over my shoulder.

"You were expecting the fashion police?"

She had thrown off her raincoat, a voluminous, battered wrapper, revealing the costume she'd walked all the way uptown from Champagne Street wearing—a man's ruffled evening shirt fastened with diaper pins, a crushed velvet cummerbund, men's longjohns dyed black and Day-Glo plaid running shoes. Fluorescent plastic skeletons danced from each ear.

She had guts. "Your tenure-track look, Luce?"

She giggled and steered me into the kitchen. "Oh, Ancient One, did you put that Puppy in the deep freeze?" I nodded. She picked up a lemon and made a cutting motion. I handed her a knife and she began to slice the lemon into translucent wafers. "Everything takes so long,"

I heard her mutter, head bent to her task. "Action, reaction, explanation, clarification. You got shot glasses?"

I handed a pair to her and she turned them admiringly under the light.

"Crystal?" She clinked them together experimentally.

I plucked them out of her hands and put them on the tray beside the lemons. She opened the fridge and stepped back, smacking a hand to her forehead in mock horror. The Black Puppy was wedged like a missile into the snow of the freezer.

"My God, Frederika, how do you all get by without a frost-free? There's barely room enough for fish sticks. Never mind, I'll fix it. I've got a method."

I carried the tray out onto the verandah. Luce pulled up a chair next to my chaise longue, kicked off her running shoes and swung her feet up onto the railing. I tried to open the bottle. Under the foil was a cap, and under the cap was a cork sealed with wax. Somebody in China had evidently gone to a lot of work to frustrate the efforts of the end-user. I extracted the cork and poured two fingers of a murky grey liquid into each glass. Luce told me to mash a slice of lemon against the roof of my mouth first, spit out the peel and knock the shot back without exhaling. The aftertaste that crawled back up my throat—socks in a locker—made the hair stand up on my arms. I gasped and slammed my shot glass onto the tray. Luce winked and poured me another.

"Eighty-proof roadkill." She motioned me to drink, downed hers and unsteadily reached over and poured us both yet another shot. We were in for an evening of it.

The muzzy body-stone washed up my spine to my brain and my thoughts began to shrink until a thousand of them could have fitted neatly on the head of a pin. Luce's hands, meanwhile, wearing her running shoes, began to cakewalk down the railing. Then, without warning, she shook her hands free, lunged forward and pulled open my shirt, exhaling in mock relief: "You *do* have tits. I was just burning to know."

I turned away and hurriedly tucked myself back in. "Real boarding-school move, Luce. Now, why don't you talk about historiography or something."

"Later, later. Wanna arm wrestle, play strip poker? How about frozen tag? I'll close my eyes and count to ten." She dropped her head, got to three and then stopped. I worried she had passed out but, no, her mouth stretched into a sly smile, her eyes opened, and she began easing her own shirt out of her cummerbund inch by inch like a conjurer until we both began giggling—and sneezing, too, for some reason. It felt good to regress, just for a night. No monks to chastise me, I couldn't resist.

"Hey, you want to hear a story?" Luce began rolling the by-now empty bottle back and forth on the table under her hand as though to massage a little more juice out of it. "The scene in Montreal is unbelievable. I mean, the clubs are fabulous!" She gave the bottle a *bon voyage* nudge and it wobbled off the table into my lap. "Women own them, women run them, just so they can stay up all night and *dance* with each other in them." She drew the word out. "You show up around eleven—"

"That's too late," I mumbled, lips numb with alcohol.

"That's early. We're talking Montreal. Bars don't really *happen* until two."

"These women have day jobs?"

"*Mais oui!* It's not a macrobiotic lifestyle, Frederika." Luce's voice was singsong with Puppy and just a trace of reproach.

"So, I'm awake. I'm at the bar. I've had my coffee. Now what?"

"Okay, we're walking into Nuit en Zoo. The bikers are there on my left, wallets-on-chains kind of women, right? Hogging the pool table, helmets and gym bags piled underneath, hats like Terry and the Pirates, tattoos, black singlets. They keep their minds on the game, very serious, money on it presumably, no eye contact with the bystanders but still to-tal-ly aware. The one waiting to play is leaning on her cue in the shadows, checking us out. Snake eyes, arms like Navratilova, six feet tall.

"No one's dancing yet but the music's enough to shake the plaster off the walls. Impossible to talk. The better to make eyes with, my dear. I finish my drink and go into the washroom to comb my hair when I stumble in on two baby dykes. You know, the ones sorta like me, with pastel brush cuts, about seventeen, everything they wear is army surplus or their granny's, bathtub-dyed black—you rub up against them, you're smudged, literally.

"Anyway, these two have treed a biker of around forty-five. The babies want to buy something which even my French can't make out. One of them runs her fingers up the biker's arm, trying to bring down the price, soften her, remind her they're all girls together. The biker's getting confused by this, her storm-trooper vibes wobbling in the face of such, uh ... generosity. The girls are wheedling: 'Give it to us, give it to us.' Then one of them turns and slips her tongue into the other one's mouth for a moment and they both burst out laughing as though it's all an act.

"The biker's totally bewildered. She wheels around to check her hair in the mirror and her eyes catch mine. Slam! Down comes her portcullis. She knows I'm not cool, just a fucking voyeur. The babes keep wheedling her and suddenly she breaks down, swaps their mon for a square of foil. The two girls fill a spoon with water and pull out a syringe. The biker leaves and I follow. Needles give me the creeps."

"Weren't you scared, Luce?"

"Of a little bit of smack? And if I was, so what? Anyway, the bar is getting so smoky my corneas are threatening to exfoliate and it's only midnight. I make for the open window but it's like an intake pipe, sucking the smoke out of the room right through my clothes. I crane my head out the window to cop some actual air but a security drone taps me and points down. It's fifty feet to the sidewalk. So what? I shrug but I shove off to the bar, order another scotch. I'm leaning against the rail, swishing my ice around and around, when I notice the bartender. She's in white from head to tail, sensational, hair buzzed short on one side and chopped into a chevron on the other. Great big hands working the suds around the glasses, rinsing them in fours, stacking them upside down in one motion, eyes fixed straight ahead. She flashes this electric smile at me, while I drink in her eyes, cheekbones, cupid mouth. We stand there, savouring our intimate conspiracy of scotch and queer love, watching the merry revelry. The dance floor is a thrash of bodies, arrayed in explicit signage, the expressions on their faces caught in flight as they pass, women entranced with one another—my cool is splitting open, pulled apart by the G-force of lust. The bartender catches it, smiles and turns back to her work.

"I park my drink and swim out onto the dance floor, feeling the heat, the stampede underfoot. I ease myself into a mass of women's bodies—this vise of flesh—my trousers rippling in the speaker wind, and it's like being swallowed by a boa constrictor.

"It's dark and too hot. I can't breathe. Claustrophobic, I tear a hole through the wall of dancers to get back out, like jumping off a carousel, the colours flitting past, strangers' body heat fanning my face. I stagger to the washroom and unbutton my shirt, twist on the cold tap, hold my head under, liking the shock of it in my ears, down my neck. I push my hair back and squeeze the duck-tail into a paper towel and see that I've wet the front of my silk shirt, it's gone transparent. When I lift it away from me and let it go, it flies to my skin like a magnet. I look into the mirror, thinking, Where the hell can I go now."

Luce was still talking when I passed out.

I woke up alone, stretched out in the chilly shadows of the verandah. The pastels of dawn were climbing the tree trunks at the bottom of the garden, glinting off the dewy spiderwebs in the grass. I sat up and tried to swallow but my tongue was as thick and dry as the finger of an old gardening glove.

My father must have walked in right past me last night without noticing—nor had I noticed him. Renie had not been impressed by my family's art of selective attention. She had called it cowardice, shaken my shoulders and told me to speak my mind, drop the shrinking-violet act.

I went into the kitchen to get a glass of water and, without thinking, reached into the freezer for an ice cube—and my fingers closed on air. The ribs of the freezer gleamed bare and dry.

In spite of the pain I tipped my head back and laughed.

＊

I began to hang out with Luce.

The following Sunday morning—after a wicked Saturday night that had culminated in a midnight croquet match, improvised with a fence picket and an old, but, as it turned out, not quite empty perfume bottle—Luce and I tottered out onto the verandah with coffee to observe the faithful strolling down the street to church. Occasionally one of them threw us a glance of disapproval but Luce waved back boldly while I smiled benignly through a blaze of headache, too hung over to care, as we passed the open thermos of coffee back and forth. I realized it had been over two weeks since I'd last meditated.

The sun, pouring through the overhanging ivy, caught a spider rappelling off the eave, its shadow looming big as an apricot against the ceiling. It braked abruptly in the air above my nose. I gave it a little tap and it scrambled up its filament of silk and vanished.

"Luce, you think time is different for a spider?"

"Starting the day off rather profoundly, aren't you? God, I've showered and I still reek of White Shoulders."

"Try tomato juice. It works for skunks."

Luce sniffed at her hands in disgust and went back to

digging at the sole of her foot with a penknife. With a grunt of pain, she squeezed the flesh until something fell into her hand. She held it out for me to see: a shard of bottle. "Got any iodine? Which reminds me. Wasn't your mum a member of the IODE?" The historiographer in her loved to excavate the subject of mothers.

From the open doors of St. Michael's, the strains of the processional hymn drifted across the lawns. I could hear the scrape of people's feet as they took their seats once again. In a moment the minister would begin.

"I used to serve tea at their meetings, occasionally, when I was a kid."

"In your impeccable frock, white ankle socks and Mary Janes, no doubt."

"I was presentable, Luce."

"Don't get defensive."

I examined the underside of that for a moment and then my eyes filled with tears, startling us both.

"Hey, Frederika."

I shook my head. "You take pleasure in miscasting me."

She indicated the direction of the church. "It's the truth, isn't it? Shaved head aside, you're halfway there. You're one of them. Destined to be crazy and rich, like your mum."

"Not true, Luce."

"No? Who gets this house? Wasn't your mother an

old girl at that boarding school of yours? They'll be holding a place for your daughter. Given any thought to kids lately? Or is it sex with women you fancy? You still haven't told me. My God, you're blushing."

"None of your business."

"Meanwhile, you're a eunuch."

"A what?"

"Oh, get real. Time you declared yourself. Give us your history, Frederika."

"It's not that simple." I stood up.

"Is there a body in the basement? Is cancer your secret? Until you tell me what you're hiding, our relationship will go nowhere. Wait. Do you think Smitty's is open? I have to eat immediately or I'm going to get really ugly."

We walked downtown in silence until we reached the diner. We ordered lunch and began quickly to eat, feigning interest at the pretty sailboards fluttering past our window.

When Luce had finished, she pushed her plate aside and took out a cigarette. "Another thing. Why do you dress so ... so virginally."

I looked down. "My topsiders?"

"My topsiders," she mimicked, lighting her cigarette, "which no one wears socks with. It's bare feet or nothing and in spite of that brush cut and T-shirt I keep hallucinating ancestral pearl studs and a twenty-four-carat charm bracelet. I bet your first eye shadow was Mary Quant—

Aha. I'm right! Look at your face. As for those—" Luce pinched her nostrils and bleated—"*Bermuda shorts* you wear, day in, day out—"

"Straight out of a *New Yorker* mail ad. Begging to be accessorized by a drip-dry Tilley hat and Bass Weejuns."

She snuffed out her cigarette in the remains of her sundae, studying me with mocking eyes as the ice cream hissed and ran black. "Gotcha," she pounced when I glanced at the people sitting opposite.

"Okay, I care. Is that so reprehensible?"

"Miss Frederika Cable sporting this season's hostess gown, a delightfully frothy confection in plaster of Paris. Hey"—she leaned in close—"depends on the cost. Loosen up, Frederika. Scream or something. Breathe."

I draped my napkin over her sundae. "I've got to go."

"Frederika," she persisted. "A guy's name, isn't it? With panties on. Face it. Your folks wanted a boy."

"Fuck off."

"Ooh, bull's-eye again. So change it."

I blinked. "To what?"

"You've never fantasized?" She dipped her fingers in my glass of water and flicked the drops into my face. "I baptize thee Freddie. Renounce the Middle Class and all Her Works."

"I am not a Freddie, Luce."

"You will be. Like Pablo's portrait of Gertrude. You will come to resemble a Freddie. Trust me."

97

_⌒_

"You're so tense. Your shoulders are up around your ears. Here, lie down." Luce patted the rug in front of the fireplace.

I was too tired to protest.

She threw me a pillow and then settled herself, kneeling, at my head. Rubbing her hands together to warm them, she undid the top of my shirt, slid it off my shoulders and began digging experienced thumbs into the ridge of frozen muscle down each side of my neck. She leaned her weight into her hands, ordering me to exhale, but the pain she caused brought only tight gasps instead. "Relax and breathe," she reminded, releasing some of her pressure as she continued searching along the muscle troughs for knots which she ground with her knuckles, shooting hot wires down my spine and out the soles of my feet. "Calcium deposits," she pronounced in a tone of aggrieved patience. "You're holding too much in. Resentment, maybe. You're working against yourself."

"Where'd you learn this stuff?"

"Part-time job last winter, bathing neurotic dogs at a veterinary clinic."

Before I had time to interpret that, she tightened her

hands around my neck, braced her knees against my shoulders and pulled on my head as though uprooting a turnip. There was a zing of pain and the bones of my vertibrae clicked audibly. I gave a whimper of dismay and she eased off. The bones slid back into alignment.

"I've cracked those deposits. You'll thank me in about an hour. Mind you, God only knows what psychic garbage I've released."

I was too tender to nod. She pressed her thumbs into nerve points where my jaw hinged, then slid them up under the ledge of each eyebrow and held until an ice cream ache poured into the sockets in turn. She moved up to the vault of my skull, seizing a tuft of hair, tugging gently on it, then taking hold of another and tugging until my scalp tingled all over. Being caressed this way, even roughly, was almost unbearably intense. I began drowning in sensations that transcended pain and entered a strange new kingdom of pleasure. I tried to resist her, flinching, but Luce pushed each shoulder down and uncurled my clenched fingers until the reptile that guarded my privacy slithered down into my belly and coiled itself up, protectively. I forced my chest to relax and took a deep breath.

My sudden surrender puzzled her. She lifted my wrist. When she let go, it dropped limply onto my stomach. She gave a grunt of satisfaction.

"That's good, thanks." I made as if to rise.

"I'm not finished," she said, pushing me down.

"No, that's okay," I said and began to struggle.

"Not yet," she said, her look fierce, and I lay back down, scowling. "It's good you resist me. Nice change from your usual passivity."

"I resent that."

"Better," she said, her smile broad.

"Now you're patronizing me."

"Why don't you lighten up just a little. Your body could use it."

She leaned over me and began to palpate down my left side and then, before I could stop her, she pulled back my shirt and this time she discovered the scars.

She sat back on her heels, staring, and then, with a finger, tentatively reached out and began to trace each chevron-shaped scar, the first, just below my breast, then the second, a hand's span below it, and the last, the tip of which disappeared under the waistband of my jeans. She measured the width of each scar with a finger, glancing to my face as she did so, then began to knead the unscarred flesh around each and the skin of my stomach broke into gooseflesh. She stroked back and forth, pressing harder and harder on the scars themselves, until the memory of how I'd made them shook me suddenly with a convulsion like orgasm. I squeezed my eyes shut and drew up a knee to fend off her probing but she was onto me, knew she'd begun to uncover what she'd been so curious about. She pinned my arm under her knee, seized my clenched left hand and forced it open to reveal the fibrous depression in the palm I'd told her was an old boating injury, and when she pressed her thumb hard into it I actually screamed and felt the burn shoot through the back of my hand.

She looked into my face, followed my eyes up the wall to a crucifix above the bookcase, the tiny wooden figure arched in agony, and suddenly she understood.

She gasped in shock and dropped my hand, sat back and stared at my side, then at the figure on the wall. Then she wiped the sweat from her lip against her shoulder and closed her eyes for a long moment, lifted my palm to her mouth, tongued it gently and pressed it against the scar on my side as though to heal one with the other.

She brought her face down close.

"Talk to me now. You did this to yourself?"

I nodded and threw an arm across my eyes.

Luce brought out the tray of tea and set it on the rug beside us.

I studied the steam swirling above the cup she handed me, exhausted by what I'd disclosed. It was the first time outside the hospital I'd told anyone those things.

"You hated opening up. Don't you feel better?"

"I guess."

"Why are you so afraid? Fear of madness is future

pain. It's the present that counts. Are you terminally intrigued by your own pacifism? Are you attracted at all to anybody? I think, in fact, you're a virgin."

"Luce!" I stopped her in alarm. What I'd just finished telling her seemed to have no impact. She was just a little girl, playing games with other people's pain. Now I wanted desperately for her to forget everything I'd told her.

"I'm not meant to have a lover of either sex. I'm a carrier."

She rolled her eyes at the word. "Maybe it's hereditary," she continued, "your indifference to passion."

Passion. I groaned, recalling my mother's wild eyes, the imaginative *luft* of her derangement, the declaration I'd overheard her make once to a supermarket clerk that each of her armpits carried the separate and distinct perfumes of coriander and sulphur, her swoops from pinnacle to abyss, the Swing Era, those manic explosions, then weeks of sepia. She had passion enough for all of us.

"You're wrong. My parents were sexual carnivores."

"See? Even the words you use—"

"King and Queen Kong. Toto and Gargantua." I beat my chest with my arms. "Beachmaster and harem. They were well matched that way."

Luce gave a twitch of exasperation. "But passion's more than that." She went over to the bookcase, took down the dictionary and began searching until she found it. "'Passion,'" she began reading aloud. "'Strong emotion. Outburst of anger; sexual love; strong enthusiasm for a thing.'"

I closed my eyes and recited. "From the Latin, *passionem*, suffering. As in the suffering of Christ on the cross."

She stared at me.

I shrugged. "Don't blame me. I didn't write it. Look, Luce, I'm trying to work out some kind of spiritual life that you seem compelled to mock endlessly while claiming to be my friend." I turned away.

Stony-faced, she slammed the book shut and put it away, picked up the tea tray and carried it into the kitchen. She came back and stood in the doorway.

"You're no holier than I am. As for the rest, I've eaten devils worse than yours for breakfast. Try being a lesbian, anywhere. You're a coward in monk's clothing. Your mother was the only one around here with the guts to be who she was."

She went downstairs. I heard the front door slam and her foot fall heavily onto the top step of the verandah. Then silence.

She had jumped over the rose bed in her haste to be gone.

～

Luce stopped calling.

Although I was accustomed to being alone and liking it, I still felt a wrench of pain each time I recalled her words—and pure loneliness. We had been seeing each other almost every day. I knew it was important not to let myself become overwrought. I meditated, worked the garden and tried to reconnect with my father, but he'd become curiously remote of late, monosyllabic, worked nights at the office, was rarely around for meals. He too seemed to prefer being a cat who walked by himself.

It was a Tuesday evening, mild wind stirring, new moon rising, but unexceptional in every way, no guardian angels, dagger-shaped clouds, red auras in the mirror or voices in the toaster to warn me of what lay ahead.

I had given up waiting for my father to come home and gone upstairs to bed when I heard his car pull into the garage. I smiled, thinking of his reaction to the note I'd left propped against the sugar bowl, an invitation for us to have lunch downtown. I waited for the creak of the garage door closing, his footsteps entering the kitchen.

Silence. The minutes crawled by. I got up and went to the window.

The garage was a dark shape against the night, the door still open. What could be keeping him out there? He always closed it before coming in. Raccoons crept in otherwise and used his banker's boxes of stored papers for a toilet. They had once fouled a decade of income-tax returns in a single night. The door was a battered metal thing that took real strength to pull down. I'd begged him to replace it with something modern, one of those remote-controlled devices.

No sign of him. Alarmed, I threw on my dressing gown, grabbed a flashlight and ran out across the lawn to the garage.

The car was parked, engine off, metal ticking as it cooled. I crouched down and flashed my light around the wheels. Nothing. Then, from inside the car I heard a squeak, muffled voices, a thump. I shone my light into the back seat and caught sight of a woman's arms wrapped tightly around my father, a sweep of stockinged calf hooked across his bare, jerking buttock.

It was something of a show-stopper for us all.

I stumbled back to the house and threw the flashlight onto the kitchen table, and with trembling hands tore up my note and began to make coffee, trying to erase what I'd seen from my memory. Renie had hinted once to me that my father might be somewhat of a ladies' man but I hadn't listened. I knew he loved my mother and he was certainly not one to rock the boat.

The pot had just begun to perk when the front door opened and I heard footsteps go upstairs. Low voices. I was setting out another cup when I heard their footsteps descend and my father came into the kitchen, face washed, hair combed, leading a woman by the hand whom, with some relief, I didn't recognize. He cleared his throat and haltingly made introductions. Her name was Susan and she was married. I didn't catch her last name.

He took a breath and continued.

Susan was vice-president in charge of public relations for Tintoretto and they were very much in love.

A spasm of giggles seized me. I covered it with a coughing fit genuine enough to alarm them both. Water was fetched and my back pounded and I was almost touched by the concern in her eyes. She turned to my father as though to ask why I was reacting this way and I threw him a look he was to describe later as Vesuvian. When I'd recovered sufficiently, I held out my hand to her in a show of civility.

We poured coffee and made herculean efforts to put one another somewhat more at ease while I did my best not to ogle the bite mark on my father's neck. His weak old heart, indeed. A flawless night of half-truths as the three of us sat adrift on an ice floe of our own contrived civility, safe as long as we sat dead centre. No sudden movements please and keep those topics light.

When I was able to extricate myself at last and escape to the solitude of my room, I sat down at my desk, picked up my pen and resolved:

1. Not to accept another cent from my father
2. To find work immediately and buy a plane ticket back to Nepal
3. Not to be seduced into discussing this with Luce or anyone else
4. To forgive my father because:

> He was a good man, community minded, virtuous, who sacrificed his own happiness for love, accepted my mother's illness without bitterness, never neglected me, was a patient teacher, generous, a good cook, a nature lover who had loved my mother and done his best to make her happy.

Or because:

> I have discovered he's just another lying, sneak-around, adulterous piece of frail, cowardly shit and therefore human after all and it's important to me not to be judgemental.

I crumpled the piece of paper into a ball, beaned it into the wastepaper basket and then sat listening to the tiny recriminating rustles as the paper relaxed, opening itself out again completely with my undaughterly words written across it for the garbage pickers of this world to read.

Had this not happened, my father and I could have floated through the summer, delusions intact. I could have flown away in the fall, he blowing kisses on the platform, my angel father, his privacy and honour preserved. Later, if things got serious between them, he could have sent me a carefully worded postcard.

What did I feel? Jealous? No. Maybe a little. Who was she to him, anyway? His co-conspirator, for one. And my mother dead only a few weeks.

That was unfair. He'd been a virtual widower for years. In point of fact, the only injured party was her poor sodding husband—and he wasn't my responsibility—but how could Dad go for someone with laquered nails and tinted hair, a *vinyl* handbag? Mother would have flipped. As for sex, he told me he'd packed that up long ago. Did Susan help him get that job? Why did I care about any of this?

With an effort, I remembered my practice: breathe in, breathe out, cultivate detachment.

Thursday. A week of awkwardness between my father and me since the garage incident. After Susan went home that night he had blasted me, called me self-obsessed, neurotic. He had shouted: Shake a leg. Do something. For God's sake, get going.

From then on we cohabited like workers on different shifts, communicating through notes taped to the fridge, vacuuming, shopping and laundering while the other was out, eating separately, retreating to our rooms. It was a challenge to us both, like swimming with handcuffs on, as though, with my mother gone, we had to manufacture domestic anxiety in order to feel at home with one another. It was familiar and so much more trustworthy than harmony.

If I'd had the money, I would have left immediately.

I began to search for Right Livelihood—work that wouldn't compromise the spiritual work I'd being doing on myself. It wasn't going to be easy to earn enough for a ticket before Christmas when the fares rose. I had not developed a single marketable skill since high school, and employment around Port Airedale was mostly seasonal, which meant layoffs in another seven weeks, so there wasn't much time. Tintoretto, I saw in the paper, was attracting post-secondary students with cash bonuses and offers of on-job training but it would have been impossible for me to work there. I checked the *Echo*'s want ads every morning and then walked downtown to the Manpower Office to scan the bulletin boards.

Nothing. A week went by. I was desperate to get my life into gear.

I was sitting at the kitchen table reading the Friday paper my father had left folded back at the classifieds when my eye caught a box midway down the page: Full-time stablehand needed at Belyea Farms. Responsible person with related experience to exercise and groom horses. Will train.

The address was a side road about twenty minutes' drive outside of town. Luckily my father had left me the car. I threw the paper onto the seat beside me and headed for the highway, too impatient to phone ahead, cursing myself for having risen so late that morning. There would probably be a lineup.

Belyea Farms, next turn. I'd seen the name on a fancy pickup truck in town once or twice but knew nothing more about the place. Horsey folk tended to keep to themselves— when they weren't talking the talk and walking the walk at local horse shows around here or down in Toronto. Handsome gates. Expensive lettering, stencilled with a rearing stallion, freshly painted, incised into cedar. I marvelled at my own eagerness for a job I should have gotten out of my system six or seven years ago.

As I rolled down the long laneway towards the house, a hound flew off the verandah and dove under my wheels. I hit the brake and slowed to a crawl, praying he'd come out again, but he only barked to assure me he was very much alive and still under my car. The dirt on both shoulders of the drive was chewed up with horseshoes, lucky U's, and in between longing for the hound to pop into view and cursing him from behind my closed window, I felt that old horsey adrenalin spurt into my stomach.

The hound's baying brought the owner out onto the verandah, a strong-jawed woman in her early forties, dusty jeans and wind-ravelled hair, who shaded her eyes with one hand in a stance that evoked a Wyeth canvas. She yelled something imprecatory at the dog and he crawled out from under, circling back towards the house with that deking, guilt-faced turn a hound can do so well.

The woman stared at me and I smiled benignly back. The lane to the farmhouse, the gingerbread trim, white-railed fence beyond, the woman, all conformed so vividly to my teenage adoption fantasy that my throat began to constrict with sadness and longing and I realized I hadn't outgrown it at all.

Never show how badly you want something. You can drive it away from yourself. A piece of advice Renie had given me.

I stepped out of the car, turned my back to the woman and took a deep breath to pull myself together.

Exhaled *one* as I slammed the car door shut. *Two*, as I turned and took my first step towards the house. *Three*, as I cupped my hand to receive the cold thrust of the hound's nose between my legs.

Her handshake was muscular and self-assured but its brevity communicated discomfort with human contact. I gave her my name and said I hoped the job was still available, trying to sound confident, neither hungry nor indifferent, pressing my trembling hands to my sides. I'd read in the Manpower Office that clients usually made up their minds whether to hire the candidate within the first three minutes of the interview. Nervousness was not an asset.

Her eyes flicked away, amused, and then returned, rinsed of expression. "You're the only one who's showed."

I hid my astonishment and beamed affably at her dog instead. Life could be wonderful. The woman asked what experience I'd had and seemed satisfied with what little I could boast of, but while I was talking a muscle under her eye began to jump and she pressed on it with her finger. I looked down and patted the hound's head until she recovered. She didn't appear to enjoy the hiring process either. Perhaps it dismayed her to consider taking on such a greenhorn.

Across the field a raven at the top of a dead pine made his cry—of water being poured up a flute. His mate answered from somewhere far off and he bent his heavy wings into circumflexes, lifted off the tree and melted into the sky. The woman smiled to herself as we watched, an inward look that reminded me of my mother's when she had been distracted. I studied her profile: strong features chiselled out of the granite of sanity. This was a woman of practical dreams, controlled flights, self-confidence, solitude. She needed no taking care of.

When she turned back to me I blinked and smiled, careful to give no indication I'd been scrutinizing her. She led me down the porch towards the barn and I noticed the heavy pair of electrical pliers in her back pocket. She told me her name was Colleen Webster, but when she saw me read the name stencilled across the roof of the barn she said: "My former husband. I was going to repaint this spring and then all hell broke loose."

I nodded, wondering what on earth she meant. She slid open the heavy door of the barn, stepped into the darkness and a ball of warmth and horse ammonia wafted out to meet me.

It was not the tidiest barn I'd seen but all the right things had been attended to. Windows filled each box stall with light. I noted automatic water bowls, blankets on each animal, feed cards neatly mounted on doors, grain bins at the end of the centre aisle. We toured the tack room. Navaho blankets, sheepskins, braided leather bridles, bosals and good saddles, English and western, had been neatly slung over trees. A nursing cat, sprawled on a grain sack, shook herself free and nudged passage between

my legs out the door. Colleen picked up one of the cali-
coes, hardly bigger than a rat, and handed it to me. I held
it to my chest for a moment, then handed it back with a
smile, remembering the strays that villagers left off at the
temple for the monks to look after or dispatch humanely,
absorbing the karma of taking life. There was a peaceful,
ordered simplicity to this barn, the promise of satisfying
manual work. I could be happy here.

She talked over her shoulder as we continued the tour.
"I've got nine horses here in boarding, plus my stallion,
Fairfax, and two mares, bred to him, who'll be foaling this
September. That makes fourteen. You smoke?"

I shook my head.

"Drink?"

"Occasionally. Never before sundown."

She grinned at that and led me down the barn to the
far end, pointing out the hot-water taps, medicine cabinet,
stocks, twitch, clippers and brushes as we went. "Where
are you living?"

"In town, with my father."

She looked at me sharply.

"My mother died this spring. I'm helping him get
through it." He would have snorted, hearing that.

"Cable, right? Didn't I read something about her?"

I nodded cautiously. "Maybe." The clippings my
father showed me had not spared many details, either of
her illness or death.

We walked back outside. "It's mostly feeding, mainte-
nance and exercising, but some riding too when I see how
you get on." She toed a horseshoe nail out of the long
grass. "I could say it's a snap job but I won't." She gave a
hoot of bitter laughter and then scowled. "It's hard work
but you'll learn about horses. I need you five days a week
and every other Saturday. A boy does the mucking out. I
pay eight-fifty a month, with a raise after six. That's my
best offer. I'll throw in board and feed if you've got a
horse. You cover farrier and vet."

She squared her shoulders and waited for my reply.

"The stallion . . . I know nothing about them."

"He's a pussycat. Don't worry."

"Okay," I said, digging for my car keys. "I'll start
tomorrow."

"Great." Her obvious relief was touching. "Six-thirty,
sharp."

We shook hands. "Freddie. . ." she mused. "Is that
with a *y* or an *ie*?"

"Whichever you like."

"Hell, it ought to matter to you."

I shrugged. "It's just a name."

I walked to my car and backed out onto the lane while
she stood watching me, making no attempt to call off the
dog, which wound tight, howling circles around my car all
the way out to the road.

It smelt like Limburger.

"Thrush," Colleen pronounced confidently and released the stallion's leg. "From standing around in damp fields." She picked up its near hind hoof, levering her shoulder under its hip to pull it higher onto her thigh. Her hoof pick dislodged what looked like the flesh of a stomped mushroom, mealy and beige. The animal swung its nose around to investigate and Colleen smacked it out of her way. "It smells worse than it is. We'll treat it and turn him out. Check it again tomorrow."

She walked around to the far leg, tugged it up by the fetlock and the animal's backside swayed towards me. Colleen had told me a rider could bring down a cantering horse just by pulling its head sharply to one side. I had seen jockey spills on TV, had once watched a politician crushed under his own horse in a rodeo accident, and I felt giddy imagining the sensation.

"Here, you do it." She threw me the pick.

I took her place and picked up the animal's foot. The stallion sighed and relaxed its penis, the flesh sliding out of its sheath, mottled and prodigious, right into my face and I choked back giggles, afraid of what Colleen would think. It seemed as though the animal was deliberately trying to swing it at me as I worked. I looked up to see Colleen grinning from ear to ear.

She took back her pick, stuck it into her pocket and moved on. I threw a cooler over the stallion and when I reached under to fasten the straps his penis had scrolled back up again.

"Horses are like sheep," Colleen mused, squinting into the setting sun as we turned them out to pasture. "They're all instinct. They spook first and ask questions later. Ever seen two stallions fight to cover a mare?"

I shook my head.

"Talk about feeling the ground move beneath you." She laughed. "You're blushing."

I spat a hay seed out. It landed on my boot. Seemed as if all people ever talked about these days was sex.

My first few days on the job were punctuated by pain and terror. My arm had almost been yanked out of its socket one morning holding back a horse startled by a sudden sun squall banging down on the barn's tin roof. Colleen's hound had a way of giving voice just as I was leading a skittish colt through a gate, and my shoulder and thigh were now blue with bruises. Occasionally, a rafter shifted overhead in the arena, making a boom like a gun going off and if I was tacking an animal up, I was left with nothing but a fistful of tail to grab on to.

Playing a fresh horse on a lunge rope in the arena, the

churn of its guts audible over the squeaking tack, I prepared myself for whatever might spook it. The first morning I brought Fairfax into the arena to lunge, a swallow swooped from the rafter with a whirr and the stallion went crazy. He reared and sprang forward, dropped his head and began to buck and snort around me like a rodeo bronc. Jerked off my feet by the rope, I flopped belly-down into the dirt, desperate, my gloved hand caught in the coils, terrified he would drag me into a rail or fall on top of me.

"Bad horse!" I yelled. "Whoa!" and Colleen appeared out of nowhere, broom in hand. "Cut him some slack!" she shouted, and I shook my hand free and rolled under the rail. Fairfax wheeled and tore up the patch of dirt I'd just been lying on. I watched the rope whip around his ears and legs, sure any moment now he would go down. I closed my eyes and began to chant.

Colleen must have done something magical because a moment later the barn went silent and it was over. She and Fairfax were together in a corner. He was shaking out his mane and nuzzling the dust around his fetlocks as though nothing at all had happened.

I wiped the dust off my cheek and swallowed. Colleen pointed me back into the ring, a little smile playing about her mouth. I climbed over the rail on rubbery legs and took Fairfax's lead from her hand.

He threw back his head when he felt my pull on him

but I spoke to him and his ears relaxed. I gave a cluck with my tongue and he broke into a trot, circling obediently. I could barely breathe for the pounding in my chest, wondering whether I still had a job, or if, in fact, I was remotely suited to this one. I halted him, winding in the lunge rope with still-trembling hands, and we stood eye to eye for a long moment.

"Not bad," Colleen said softly, coming up beside me. She cupped the stallion's chin in both hands and breathed deliberately into his nostrils. "You try it." The stallion returned a surprisingly soft, long exhalation, hay-fragrant, warm and moist. "Never panic. It's a waste of time." Colleen took the rope from my hands. With a cluck she sent Fairfax circling, lengthening the radius as she fed him rope, showing me how to direct his flanks outward with the lunge whip while not slowing him down or touching him, ever. She handed me the rope and headed for the rail.

"Read his ears. They'll tell you plenty. It's not knowing that gets you into trouble."

Lunging him turned into pure choreography after that, dizzying at first to follow his circles until, like a dancer, I learned to spot a fixed landmark from time to time, keeping the circle large and centred, not dimpling in towards me as we travelled or bulging at the corners, pushing his blurred form away from me with my whip, bracing my heels against the pull, arm stinging all the way up to the shoulder, clucking to keep the *tick-tock* pace of hoofbeats consistent, not running down like a clock whenever he passed the exit gate, by raising my whip arm just high enough to reinvoke the I and Thou distinction, wriggling the lash through the dirt, snakelike, whenever he threatened to drift in too close. The radius between us springing taut, sagging, springing taut again.

By the third week, I found I no longer needed words to monitor what I was doing and I began to work purposefully towards that recognition. I found my eyes and ears taking in more, my body sensing what came next. Being more in my body, less in my mind. The fear began to slack off. Colleen's taciturnity now seemed natural, not some deficiency or effort at concealment. I envied her, wished I could be more like her, such a capable, pragmatic woman, so self-possessed. I wondered where her dreams took her at night.

The dying sun glinted off the bumper of my parked car as I stepped out into the yard one day after work. Before I could catch myself I had swept my hand across the car's flank, warning of my approach from behind.

My peal of tight laughter ricocheted off the side of the barn, scattering the crows into flight, black knots against the sky.

I am scaling the fridge, climbing like a fly into the freezer to search for food while she sits rocking far below at the kitchen table, talking furiously to herself. I drop onto the stove, unlit gas hissing from each burner, my mother's cheeks puffing as she leans forward and blows out each pilot like a birthday candle, her eyes triumphant, my lungs filling with the rotten-egg smell, eyes stinging. I'm taking too long, getting dizzy, fumbling with the matches, the whole box spilling over my feet which are bare, I'm terrified one will light the river of gibberish pouring from her mouth, I cover my ears shutting it out, then remember I want to get us both someplace safer but I can't pull her up from her chair, she's so heavy and sliding around inside her clothes making a game out of it, I'm frantic clutching handfuls of empty cloth shrieking at her to grow up and help me.

I awoke crying, my bedroom as hot and claustrophobic as a coffin. A faint breeze moved my curtain aside, the current barely detectable against my skin, the wake of a flying insect. I got up and splashed cold water onto my face, trying to relieve the pressure that was building inside my skull.

I drove to work with the windows down and the radio turned up loud. The weather report called for rain but the sky was cloudless with a low, red sun that burned through my shirt. I threw myself into yard work, raking out the paddock, hosing down the barn walls, trying to shake off the dread that was creeping over me again, despite my mother's death, of the Swing days of August when her mental state deteriorated, the depression giving way to florid delusions and sometimes violence, until inevitably we had to hospitalize her, which she hated. My grandmother, her mother, had also tended to destabilize around this time of year. Anticipating her own mother's condition may have contributed to her stress and, now, I too seemed to have inherited this seasonal anxiety. Was it only habit or the emergence of a pathology? Best not to think about it.

I led the horses out into the yard and hosed them down with warm cistern water, their hair parting, silvery hide beneath, then turned them out into the field to twitch dry. At five o'clock, grateful for day's end, I eased myself onto the car's scalding upholstery and started for home. I was fiddling with the dial and had just tuned into a country-and-western station from Arkansas, of all places, a fluke occurrence this far north, when a fancy pickup truck with a punched-out brake light pulled onto the road in front of me, raising such a cloud of dust I had no choice but to roll the windows up and suffocate or leave them down and suffocate.

When I dropped back, the pickup truck did too and I spotted a rifle in his cab rack. Anxious to get away, I pulled out to pass but he swerved over the centre line, cutting me off. Coming over a hill I had another opportunity but he was watching in his rear-view and blocked me again. Sweat trickled down the back of my neck. There wasn't another car around for miles, no phones, no gas stations. Suddenly he veered off onto the shoulder, his one good brake light glowing through the dust like a villain's cigar. Was he inviting me to pass? I gave him the finger instead, palmed the wheel around sharply and headed back the way I'd come. The road of life was too short to share with assholes like this. I hit the gas, surprised at my own decisiveness. I'd stop back at Colleen's for a while, cool out, have a beer, hit the road again. I stretched out my clutch leg and gave a sigh of relief but to my horror he pulled out after me, grinning like a demon and flashing his headlights. For a second I deeply regretted my finger and wondered whether he would actually ram me. I gunned my father's old Chev and prayed it didn't rupture a ventricle as Arkansas disintegrated into skritchy popcorn.

When I reached Colleen's laneway I cut the corner and swerved in on two wheels, throwing up a cloud of dust that, to my dismay, the pickup drove straight into, following tight behind me all the way to the barn.

I yanked the key from the ignition, got out and turned

to face him, having no idea what came next. Through his filthy windshield I could make out his face, a not bad-looking man in his mid-forties, bearded, wearing a new summer Stetson. Over my shoulder I yelled for Colleen and stared hard at him with the toughest look I could conjure, heart pounding, counting the seconds before I could yell for her again. Where was that damn dog when you needed him. The cowboy sat there in his cab, grinning, one arm draped across his side mirror, enjoying the look on my face.

I heard the screen door slam. Before I could get the words out to warn her, Colleen had walked right over to the truck and ordered him out, asking him what the hell he meant by driving in here like that, throwing up enough dust to choke her horses, and did he intend to stick around long enough for coffee or what?

I was stunned. Colleen had told me her ex-husband was out west somewhere, doing time for a string of petty B and E's. He pointed a lazy finger towards me and gave a cutesy little wave that made me want to run for the phone but Colleen seemed almost to be flirting with him. I'd never seen her act so girlish. She brushed his arm lightly, trying to persuade him to accept her invitation, and plucked at her hair. He appeared to weigh her invitation for a moment and then he shook his head, pulled his arm inside and, saying something too low for me to catch, leaned out to kiss her cheek.

Colleen let fly an expletive. The man jerked back as though she'd slapped him, shrugged and then began, deliberately, to roll his window up in her face. Colleen hooked her fingers over the glass and then saw she would lose and withdrew them. The man inside laughed and she hit at his face, hard, through the window.

At that, the hound cleared the porch rail in one liquid movement and bounded protectively to Colleen's side, throwing his forepaws up against the door of the cab with a snarl. Whether he recognized the man or not I couldn't tell but the truck had already begun to roll forward. Colleen walked alongside, hitting the window with both fists now, the hound barking beside her, but the man only laughed again behind the glass, pulled his hat low and accelerated past them, leaving Colleen to stare after him as he turned onto the highway and disappeared.

I fought an impulse to run, resenting her weakness, her coquetry around such a man, afraid she would turn around next, stretch out a hand to me, plead for my help. "Frederika? Need you. Just for a moment."

It was Susan's first dinner at our house, and not five minutes after I'd finished setting the table my father rearranged it, moving Susan to my mother's place, which I'd left empty, opposite him. I felt a twitch of dark displeasure.

Susan arrived early, mutton dressed as lamb in a padded rhinestone-and-black-denim suit, hair up in combs, lacquered talons gripping a bottle of quite good French champagne by the neck, warming the gases so that the cork was sure to go through the ceiling. My father embraced her with one arm, mouth on hers, swinging the bottle underhand to me, his minion—a move he'd picked up from a Ronald Colman flick we'd watched together the previous weekend. Susan's slit skirt flashed open to reveal an acreage of well-tanned thigh. She wore one of those magazine-ad perfumes that I discovered had come off the champagne bottle onto my hand. I put the bottle down and went into the kitchen to wash it off but soap and water only seemed to spread it across both hands and now the towel which I threw in disgust under the sink.

I walked back into the dining room a minute later to discover them nuzzling, my father's hands busy under her jacket. I felt like a kid in the back seat at a drive-in, all the

126

more so in my jeans and hooded sweatshirt, sexless and ugly. I didn't know where to look.

"What do we plan to do about dinner?" I made no attempt to filter the annoyance from my voice.

My father cocked a Colmanesque eyebrow at me. "What's to do? Pizza's in the oven—half vegetarian, remember? My Buddhist monk of a daughter can sleep with a clear conscience tonight." He grinned at Susan.

My cheeks flared. He was deliberately making me look stupid, showing off in front of her, betraying me. For starters, the pizza had been my idea.

"Anyone for champagne?" Susan clicked her fingers close to her ears like castanets.

"Right!" My father bounded to the table, plucking up glasses, the bottle and a napkin while Susan and I stood there, staring at each other's hair. Instead of bracing the bottle against his chest he sat down and planted it, suggestively, between his closed thighs. Susan dropped down in front of him to help, seizing hold of the neck in both hands. They both looked at the bottle and began sniggering like adolescents.

"Good grief." They looked up at me, startled. "Heavens, don't stop on my account." They traded glances, nonplussed. A pinpoint of rage and misery began to burn between my eyes. "In fact, let me help." Before my father could stop me I began flipping through record albums until I found my mother's favourite, set the needle down at the first song and slid the volume bar to the top until the piercing clarity of the Sisters grew punitive. "Don't sit under the apple tree with anyone else but me," I sang. "Let's see you two dance, come on."

I could feel my mouth tighten, my eyes wide and unblinking, and I knew I looked as demented as I felt. The fright on my father's face was giving me particular pleasure, liberating more anger. I snatched the needle off, dropped it again onto the next song with a casual precision so like my mother's, despite trembling hands, that I was astonished. "Alone Again." A minute of that and then on to "One Mistake," "Crazy Arms" and "Rum and Coca-Cola." I could hear my mother's own clear contralto, could smell her smoky hair. My father was shouting at me but I was too busy gathering up albums in my arms to listen. I took a step towards him and Susan instinctively threw an arm out. "Widower!" I shouted. The second time I said it I shoved the records hard into his stomach. "Can't stand the heat, get out of the kitchen," I exploded at Susan—and was suddenly empty. I had nothing in my hands, nothing in my head left to say, felt nothing at all except a desire to escape and lie down, away from their eyes and that music. I intended to go upstairs to my room but, instead, found myself walking straight into the kitchen, of all places, truly a dead end, having no idea why I was there or how to get past them again to my room.

The pizza. *Yes.* A task. Food. Maybe the smell of it

had led me here. I went over to the stove but my arms wouldn't move. I was listening to people at the far end of the house having an argument. A woman's voice, not my mother's, was remonstrating. I heard her utter my name and my forehead began to throb again, the force behind the champagne cork, urgent, expanding, needing out. I felt that familiar, unbearable ache to do something, *quick*, to myself, alleviate the pressure before it ripped my brain apart. I knew this feeling by heart and the way to cure it at least for a while, and I began jerking open drawers, searching for a tool to use. It always came just before, this pressure. It felt exactly like the feeling of needing sex. I sat down hard on the floor.

Susan found me there, with my back against the cupboards, knives and forks spilled across my lap, staring into space. She touched my shoulder gently. I looked into her face. "I've made a mess of things, haven't I."

She smiled slowly. "You've mostly made a mess of yourself." She lifted the cutlery drawer off me. "Do you mind if we talk?"

I shook my head, no longer sure what I minded any more.

She slid down to the floor beside me. "Maybe I can help."

"Wait. Where's my dad?"

"He's okay. I sent him outside for a stroll so we could have some privacy."

In my mother's house are many mansions: if it were not so, I would have told you. I go to prepare a place for you.

I had thought it would be simple. I would come home, help my father bury my mother, stay with him until the traffic of mourning had died away and his life was on track once more, earn some money and be gone.

Nothing was working out the way I had expected.

I phoned Colleen and asked for the day off, then threw lunch and a map into the car and drove a hundred and twenty miles in the opposite direction to the psychiatric hospital, one of my mother's many mansions during her years with us. The last time I'd gone to visit my mother had been a grey, bleak morning, five years earlier, during Christmas week. There was always such a forlorn, dismal feeling to the place at that time of year—the crunch of salt underfoot on the path from the parking lot, the enforced festivity, honeycomb crepe-paper bells over the doorways, dusty reindeer taped to the wire-glass doors, snowflake mobiles I had to duck to get past, and everywhere only the sickest of patients, and the most surly of staff, resentful at having been left behind.

I could feel my back tighten again as I pushed open the front doors, bracing myself for the sour-milk stench of stale sweat and body ash given off by incarcerated souls but, miraculously, despite the heat and close air, there was almost none. Instead, there was air conditioning and fresh flowers on the reception desk. A man at the end of the corridor was industriously swabbing down the floor with what smelled like pine balm and my first weeks at the temple came back to me. I admired his mop's calligraphy for a moment and then, remembering what I'd come for, turned down the other corridor in search of my mother's doctor, hoping he might talk to me, let slip something new about her, something that might reassure me about her illness. I was also hoping, this visit, to find someone else to talk to, a nurse, a fellow patient maybe, someone who'd been her friend and could share some stories.

The doctor, once I'd tracked him down between rounds, was sympathetic but he refused to divulge information about his former patient, even to me, or to predict my future beyond citing some statistical percentages he thought comforting and expressing confidence that early diagnosis and promising new medications were the best defence against her particular, et cetera. He did, however, give me one gift in parting: the names of three women on a ward two floors above who'd been inseparable friends of my mother.

The moment I walked through the ward doors I saw

clearly which ones he meant. Three old ladies locked in
the lavatory. They were hunched over cards at a table
under the window, cardigan sweaters draped over their
shoulders, hair in forties-style perms, the only ones in the
room wearing lipstick. My mother would have made the
fourth.

They looked up from their cards, saw me, or more
precisely saw the stack of magazines I had bought for
them in the tuck shop, and, nudging one another, stared
with such carnivorous intensity at what I carried that I
laid them down immediately on their table, the one with
the photograph of Lady Diana topmost.

A shiver of anticipation—but not one of the women
made a move yet to touch the magazines. I studied their
cards as I searched for some kind of opener. They
appeared to have created a kind of three-handed gin
rummy but were using a cribbage board to keep score.
There were also two different decks in use although no
one seemed to notice. I stopped worrying about making a
formal introduction and simply motioned to the magazines. "Help yourselves."

Instantly the cards fell and there was a flurry of hands
clawing, two audible slaps, a tug-of-war, the sound of
paper ripping and it was over. Each of them had three
magazines. A strip off Lady Di's head fluttered to the
floor.

"Whadyoucomeherefor?" It was out of the speaker's

mouth so fast I couldn't tell which one had spoken. All three stared at me, awaiting my response.

"Well, my mother was a patient here for a long time...."

"Ohweknowthat, weknowthat." It was the tiny one in the middle, with glittering birdlike eyes and yellow hair, her tone peevish. Her voice went up an octave and she sang: "Filled with a grief she could never, ever name." Her voice dropped back to normal again. "I know you. We all know you, plain as day. Look at your hands. You're Isabel's girl." The women on either side glanced over and nodded corroboration as they flipped through their magazines.

"Then you know my name."

She squinted at me. "Fa-red-e-rika. Show us your scars, come on, come on."

Taken aback, I put my left hand into hers. She turned it over, touched the place, winced theatrically and let my hand drop.

"I'm Josephine. This is Mrs. Parrish"—she nodded left—"and this"—she nodded right—"is Daphne. We're lifers."

I nodded to each of them in turn.

"Your mother told us plenty about you. Plentyplentyplenty." Josephine closed her eyes and sighed. Then she began to recite: "Five foot eight, right-handed, brown hair and eyes, shoes eight and a half, one hundred and twenty pounds, born September eight, thus a Virgo, eighteen sixty-nine."

"Nineteen sixty-nine," I corrected.

Her eyes shot open. "One, eight, six, nine." She pronounced each number separately. "One eight six nine one eight six nine one eight six nine one eight six nine. Izzo's in heaven now."

Izzo? I'd never heard that before. A nickname.

"We made the doctors talk but we knew the moment she died. We all knew it. We miss Izzo." Suddenly she sang: "Her little life rounded with a sleep. Pay attention, you!"

She sounded just like Teacher. The others began murmuring a rondo of "Miss Izzo, Miss Izzo," like bees in a garden, and I felt myself becoming almost narcotized by them. I shook my head, wanting control back. "So you are the ones who knew Izzo best?"

At that, they each began talking at once about Izzo this and Izzo that, vying for my attention until Josephine raised a hand as though to smack them and they fell back mute. She turned to me and began to sing the opening bars of a song, all rhythm and huff, the tune askew, but with a start I recognized "Six Jerks in a Jeep," one of my mother's favourites. The Sisters had followed her here. Daphne and Mrs. Parrish listened impatiently until finally when the chorus came around again they couldn't stand it and they jumped up, pushing their chairs aside.

To the amusement of the rest of the ward, they launched into what looked like a pantomime of folding laundry until I realized they were dance steps. Josephine wound up the song and, breathless and flushed, the dancers flopped back into their chairs, fanning their cheeks, as Josephine began a rambling chain of anecdotes about my mother, the others warming to their task of contradicting and cutting in until a garbled and baroque but curiously distinct portrait of my mother began to emerge, iridescent around the edges with the mental peculiarities of its creators—at times I felt sure I was half-dreaming a way through to coherence—but I could definitely see someone new—a woman who had woven an almost sane friendship among those around her, sharing her songs, teaching them to fox-trot, styling Mrs. Parrish's hair the day her nephew came to visit, making a funny game out of the various medical procedures. *By the pricking of my thumbs, something wicked this way comes,* she incanted whenever the ECT team appeared on the ward.

She had also shared with them absolutely everything about me—showing them photographs, my school report card, boasting about my riding lessons, my birthday parties, my piano recital. These women knew when I'd gotten my first period, passed my driver's test. Like blind women feeling a camel, each laid claim to a different creature, but they shone with such pride in the particulars of their knowledge that, for the first time, I felt my mother's pride in me too and my shame began to roll back like a mist.

She had endured much in this place. I didn't know how she had borne it. To these women she was heroic and her madness less absolute, less fearful to me than before. I understood something of the comfort and security this place had provided her. Her history was not so different from my own, of attraction and repulsion to places of retreat.

"You went where?" He sat down heavily at the kitchen table and dropped his head in his hands. With a sigh, he rubbed his face and pushed back his hair.

"It wasn't so bad." I put a cup of coffee down in front of him. "In fact it was good. I met some of her friends."

He sniffed at the word and for an instant I wondered if in fact he was jealous. "Luce put you up to this?"

"Dad, I thought you and I had agreed to put our guns down and talk. No, she didn't."

He began to stir his coffee. "Your obsession with your mother's illness worries me. I have to say that. She's gone. Couldn't you put her behind you?"

"I'm working on that."

"Your friend Luce doesn't come around much any more. Is she afraid of me or something?"

"Afraid? No, we're just taking a break from each other."

"She pressure you? I mean, she's a lesbian, isn't she?"

"We're good friends, as it happens, not lovers. But I hope you'd accept it if we were."

"That's a howl, coming from you."

I looked down.

That night I decided to phone Luce. She was out, so I left a message with her grandmother, telling her I missed her and would like to talk.

I opened the door at the top of the stairs and listened. The banging sounded as though it was coming from the laundry room, old sanctuary of my mother's. In spite of the lightness I felt after making friends with Susan, I experienced an involuntary shiver, hating, even now, to go down there. I would hide in my room and do homework while she holed herself up below, hunched over her radio, lost among the plots of the late-afternoon soaps, furiously chain-smoking Gauloises as she flipped through stacks of her women's magazines, tearing out whatever caught her fancy—a photo of a movie star's dishevelled deathbed, a home recipe for a depilatory, anguished letters to an advice columnist in Washington whose responses were marvels of callous brevity: Wake up, sister, and smell the coffee.

One winter she was obsessed by things British and clipped a series of obscure political cartoons from the *Manchester Guardian*. These she pasted to the walls, together with whatever other printed matter caught her magpie eye—a hand-tinted portrait of Jesus knocking on a thorn-choked heart that I'd brought home from Sunday school, movie ticket stubs, if she'd liked the flick, a Chinese take-out menu, for the calligraphy. When she ran out of wall space, she climbed onto the washing machine and began pasting across the ceiling until that too was covered, several layers deep in places. She disguised the taps of the laundry tub with aluminum foil, draped her pirate scarf across the window, blotching the room a psychedelic paisley.

My father and I, doing the Saturday wash together, would pore over the walls, pondering each addition as though hoping one day we might crack the code of my mother's hieroglyphic nature.

The banging was definitely coming from the laundry room. I sighed and forced myself downstairs and into the laundry room.

Nothing had changed, not even the scarf. The clippings were discoloured with mildew but still legible and, automatically, I began to scan for the newest addition. The banging's source was a window over the laundry tubs that had blown open. I climbed up onto the dryer to close it and there was her old ashtray, a Limoges saucer hidden behind the curtain, chipped and tar-blackened. I picked it up and inhaled—her hair, her sweaters, the two fingers of her right hand. I put it back and jumped down, anxious suddenly to be out of the room, feeling her presence with a melancholy that made my temples tighten. I closed the door behind me.

The basement walls were lined with shelves of preserves representing one extraordinary summer orgy of pickling and preserving during which my mother reduced fields and berry bogs to jam and jelly. Vats of tomatoes, cucumbers, cauliflowers, raspberries, gooseberries, red and black currants, a mountain of shredded orange and lemon peel, their seeds soaking in hot water to extract the pectin—no artificial thickeners for her!—were blanched, stewed, salted, boiled or puréed until the walls of the kitchen ran with sticky water. Our hair, our bedclothes, the upholstery, the woodwork, even the wallpaper itself absorbed the odours of her concoctions. Overcoats and sweaters brought out of closets that fall released a cloistered fragrance of ginger, chili, onions, dill, vinegar.

She gave cartons of her bounty away to neighbours, people from church, her IODE-ers, but the sheer volume of her generosity eventually overwhelmed them and they grew wary of her approach, flinched at the clink of jars in bags, hid behind their blinds, left the doorbell unanswered.

As though to punish us all for this rejection, she redoubled production and my father was obliged to throw up additional basement shelving to divert the flow of mason jars away from the main floor of the house, he and I having come to an understanding, following her woollen phase, never again to cede the territories of living room, dining room or hall.

October arrived, and mercifully with it the decline of

the Swing Era, as well as the dwindling of preservable foodstuffs. Fruits and vegetables from California were far too expensive to buy in bulk, and by then my mother had fallen under the influence of a Swiss publication advising readers against consuming foods grown too far from home: too many preservatives, too many unnatural agricultural practices, too much produce shipped green, then forcibly ripened with gases in dark chambers to be digested out of season by stomachs unprepared with the appropriate enzymes. These and other naturopathic admonitions were clipped and pasted to the walls of the laundry room, together with cryptically discreet ads for high-colonic purgatives. By winter, our consumption of preserves had undergone a revisionist evaluation. Vinegar was now suspect. My mother made us swear off all but the marmalades and chutneys which were now expected to accompany every meal. It gave her such pleasure to see the bottles on the table that we complied without grumbling although we had trouble stomaching certain combinations—fruit compote with pasta, especially.

I walked down the rows of dusty jars, peering into the rich, unrecognizable gloom of their contents, calculating the hours she had spent in their production, and idly began searching for a chutney to go with the curry I'd planned for dinner. The metamorphosis of my mother's handwriting was traceable on the curling labels, careening from a loopy, sophomoric script on her early efforts to the crabbed Sanskrit that characterized her later years.

While I'd been away in my temple she had come down and rearranged each shelf by colour: a band of vermilion chili sauce gave way to the purple splendour of beets, the diluted gold of marmalade above that.

I began pushing jars aside, reading their dates, stacking them at my feet, hunting for the fleshy tint of a peach chutney, wondering whether, in fact, any of it was still edible, when my fingers closed on a tiny little bottle tucked down in behind the others. I pulled it out, light as dust, its contents dessicated, rattling, dry as peas.

I tilted it under the light.

Baby teeth.

My own. The complete set, according to the label. She had collected them, one by one, the tooth fairy, caching them all these years. Pasted under the lid was a tiny photo and the word: *baby*. She was holding me in my christening robes against her shoulder on the front steps of our church, squinting into the sun at the photographer, probably my father, judging by her expression of unchecked pride, but behind her eyes was a shadow of the darkness she had already begun to suppress.

A gift from her at last. This preserved kiss of farewell to me.

～

Luce flung our packs into the bow of the canoe, slid the
cooler under the middle thwart, fitted the tent alongside,
more gear, her sweater, my raincoat. She settled herself in
the bow with a grunt and I took the stern.

"Tents and sleeping bags, greasy hair, half-cooked
food. All the comforts of home. Why are we doing this,
Freddie?"

"Didn't you go camping as a kid? It's a long winter
ahead. Besides, it's a great way to catch up."

"Okay, then let's really rough it. No tent, no clothes,
just a knife, matches and a fish hook, smear ourselves with
mud—uh-oh, rock ahead. Hard to port."

I jerked my paddle and the bow swerved left. Luce
whistled through her teeth as we came alongside a boulder, striped with paint scraped off previous hulls.

We paddled on in silence.

Luce's tent was one of those spring-loaded, self-
erecting jobs that, released from its bag and shaken,
lurched to its feet like a camel. We kicked off our shoes
and crawled inside. The late-afternoon light through the
bright nylon tinted our skins Popsicle orange, our veins
purple, and when our sleeping bags were spread out I

couldn't tell which was whose, the colours were so distorted. We lay on our backs watching the leafy shadows play across the walls, letting our tired muscles unkink, the feathers of silent forest wafting down around us. I rolled my sweater into a ball under my head and closed my eyes, anxious not to reopen any more subjects. I had almost dozed off when I became aware of being scrutinized. I opened an eye. Luce, propped up on one elbow, was staring down at me.

"Thought we could nap a bit, Luce."

She shrugged. "I'm not tired."

I sighed. "Something you need to say?"

"Something I need to do." She rolled on top of me and slid her tongue into my mouth. We began to kiss, her hands sliding up inside my sweatshirt, her knee parting my legs to slide between. I touched her thin back, feeling each fragile bone—she was greyhound thin. I seized a fistful of her hair, her little ducktail, and gently tugged it. When she caught my lip between her teeth I gasped and she pulled me on top of her and we rolled over and over, wedging ourselves finally against the mound of our backpacks as hard and unbudgeable as a boulder.

Luce sat up and looked around, indignant. "This fucking tent has shrunk!"

I couldn't help it. I began to laugh, tipped my head back until I began to choke on waves of laughter. Then Luce surrendered to it too.

I cleared my throat. "Luce, I mean I feel all kinds of things for you but not this. This is silly."

She wiped her eyes, sat blinking for a moment. "Well, we tried. We definitely did our best."

"We did and it could have been great."

"A little farmhouse together somewhere, a horse for you, chickens for me, buckskin curtains, snowshoes over the mantel. Like something out of Willa Cather. I'd never have to do another family Christmas. You'd be free of Airedale's expectations—baa baa black sheep." She sang happily, her body loose.

"You're not disappointed?" I ventured, not yet daring to trust this new ease between us.

"That we have zero chemistry?" She shrugged. "It surprised me briefly. But nah. You?"

I shook my head. "We are definitely attracted to something about one another, though."

She raised a finger. "Clearly outside the sexual realm."

I went down to the river bank, stripped and dove in. The opaque jelly of warm water closed over my eyes and plugged my ears and I wanted to stay under forever. I swam blind until I'd dribbled out the last of my air and had to kick to the surface, rolling over and over like a dolphin.

Frederika.

My mother's voice!

Lost to me for so long, it sounded sweet, like a bird's,

sending shivers across my heart. Was I dreaming?

I treaded water and held my breath, waiting, but it didn't return. I began to shiver and pushed on, replaying her voice until I'd distorted it beyond recall.

When I came to a long bend in the river I stood up in the sunny shallows and waded for a bit, the water eddying under my armpits. I took a step and sank into cold mush, liberating bubbles of swamp gas that wobbled to the surface and broke under my nose. I drew my feet up, swam a few strokes, then let them drift back down in search of sandy bottom, making an effort not to conjure up thoughts of her again.

I walked and swam downstream for some time that way. The river bent around again and eventually I noticed I'd put the sun behind me and began to calculate how far back I'd left our encampment, mindful of reserving enough strength for my return, but the warmth of the water, the yoke of cool air across my shoulders, the feeling of something hovering in wait for me around the next bend made me yearn to turn back but I couldn't.

No one is born knowing how.

Her voice again! Spoken right into my ear. Even in the water I jumped. The librarian of my heart's keeping had fetched this sentence back unbidden and with it the occasion when I had first heard it:

A day or so after Christmas, on this same river, the black ice swept clear of snow. My mother, bending to lace up my skates, pulling me to my feet, etched into the ice around us an elegant chasery left by her blades, figure eights and spirals where she had spun and twirled, swooped to the end and back, braked dramatically in front of me, spray arcing off her blades, impatient to impress me, teach me everything she knew while there was still time.

Water was moving under the ice. I couldn't do it. Strings of dirty trapped bubbles, dark shapes in the crumpled reeds below. Like walking on top of water. I clutched her tight, wailed out my fear.

Frederika, let go of my hand.

What was happening? Was I going to go crazy in this river? I dove to the bottom, filling my mouth and ears with mud, kicking out at whatever brushed against me, lungs burning, thrashing and tumbling in the darkness, willing my mouth to open, take the water in.

I couldn't, not that way.

I gave a kick and thrust up, chest about to split open, fist squeezing my heart as I broke the surface and the airy world roared back into my eardrums. I gasped and looked up. The whole strenuous activity of burrowing out endless refuges was false. It hadn't worked for my mother and it wasn't going to work for me. In that instant, I understood I was responsible for my own suffering—and therefore my happiness. Something broke inside. I'd feared and envied my mother's power for so long, blamed her illness for so much, set up attraction-repulsion forces between us so strong I could hardly draw breath against them.

As I swam back, I lifted my head to get my bearings off the blur of ferns along the bank, and other words, spoken so long ago, coursed back with each stroke:

These things take time.

I broke free. Glided into the larger world.

I pulled myself out, trembling and cold, onto the bank of our encampment and walked on rubbery legs out of the shadows to stand panting by the glow of Luce's fire, drops falling from my hair with little hisses onto the coals like drops of blood.

"Frederika! What took you so long?"

Something in my face stopped her saying more. She handed me the thermos instead and I squatted and poured out a cup of hot milky tea, my fingers numb to the metal, nails gone grey with cold. Luce fetched my sleeping bag and a towel out of the tent and I rubbed myself dry, then wrapped the bag around me and poured another cup of tea.

"You okay?"

I cleared my throat. "I think so. I'll tell you in the morning." I smiled. "I promise."

Luce pulled two burning logs apart with her hand, wedged a fresh one into the space between. A column of flame shot up into the sky and for an instant our faces were lit up, bright as day.

It was two o'clock. I had offered to drive Luce to the train
station. I turned down Champagne Street and pulled up
outside her grandmother's cottage. Through the screen
door I could see Luce wrestling with the lid of her suitcase. Together, we sat on it and pressed the clasps shut.

She glanced around the room distractedly. "I've got
my cash, my ticket, left my note to Granny. This has definitely got to be my last year of school. I can't afford to
drag out my degree any longer."

We had been over this already. "You'll get it. You're so
close."

She looked at me. "You're right. Positive attitude.
Ignore these preregistration butterflies. You know"—she
dragged her suitcase off the bed towards the door—"in
retrospect, I've had a good summer."

I nodded. "It's been good."

We swung her bag into the trunk of the car. Already,
the first of September, a sharp tang of autumn was in the
air and we both wore sweaters. The rows of ministry-
planted firs on either side of the highway flitted by with
dull regularity, broken only by the occasional errant
birch, flush of crimson and gold foliage through the

gloom of green. Misfits abounded, even in nature.

Luce's brow was furrowed. She bit her thumbnail.

"I'll write, wherever I am, Luce. I promise."

She sighed. "I just have this ridiculous problem with leave-taking. I get tragic and superstitious—I mean, if a bird hit our windshield I'd read all kinds of—"

A damsel fly exploded across the glass with a *phut*, leaving a neat, yellow exclamation mark on Luce's side.

"Oh, mercy."

"Luce, there isn't time to pull over and perform last rites."

"No, no. Ignore me. It's a flaw I have, overinvesting such moments with significance."

"I wouldn't know anything about that."

"Which reminds me. What's happening with your dad?"

I smiled. "Things are good now. Maybe better than they've ever been for him. We're in touch these days. Susan helps."

"No more evasions?"

"What, and topple years of tradition? Home wasn't built in a day."

She groaned.

The highway widened as we came to the turn-off.

"Where are you going first, Freddie?"

"I don't know." I pulled up in front of the station. We got her bag out and stood at the doors. When we hugged

I could feel the knobs of her spine through the sweater. The people in my life seemed perennially underweight. "Eat more croissants this year, okay? Mail me the crusts for proof. I love you, Luce."

"Me too. I mean—you know."

She wiped her nose and ordered me not to wait, turning one last time to blow me a kiss and then she was gone.

I drove straight through town to the dock, threw back the tarpaulin of my father's launch and started up the motor, driving at half throttle until I'd left the harbour behind me, and with some rope rigged up a pulley arrangement with the steering wheel so I could ride and steer from the bow of the boat and hang my feet over the side, watching them fly over the clouds reflected below. The wind blew my sleeves into spinnakers, flattened my hair, and I caught traces every now and again of the intense watery smell that indicated fish close by.

An underwater forest of grey vegetable stalks appeared out of nowhere under the keel, angling up towards the light, barely clearing the outboard's skeg. I'd driven into a maze of shoals. I lunged for the throttle, pushing it down, as a shelf of granite, not six inches below the surface, appeared out of nowhere. I jerked the wheel and the launch veered away with a shudder as the hull dragged across. I cringed, anticipating the *ting* of the prop blade shearing off, dreading the thought of a dive, but I was lucky this time. I slipped the motor into neutral, raised it and punted through the shoals using an oar until I had reached deep water again.

I headed the boat due east, straight into the wedge of light where water met the sky. The lighthouse on Snake Island, its peeling shingles bleached the colour of an old life preserver, stood on an arm of pink granite, soft and curved as flesh. Herring gulls, gilded in the late-afternoon light, wheeled above, screaming and diving, jostling for a perch along the spine of roof sagging with generations of their droppings.

An upwelling of sadness. Death-ache and loneliness, right through to my bones.

I nudged the wheel a couple of degrees west, putting the island behind me, the bow rising to meet the wind, and looked back to the hump of Belvedere Hill where my parents' house stood, downtown to the flags of the shopping mall, the lumber stacks, the warehouses, the propane tanks, the railway sidings, to where the Tintoretto stack stood, white and sparkling, like the handle of a shiny new screwdriver, tightening up the future of the town, an answer to its people's prayers.

So be it.

Ahead of me the other islands rose up like humpbacks for as far as the eye could see, a landscape indifferent to the calamities larding the hearts of all the humans who had ever entered it. I could no more entertain delusions of my own permanence here than could the weather itself.

I cut the motor and drifted. When the boat was steady again I stood up on the bow and, reaching into my shirt, took out the envelope and shook my mother's ashes into a mouth of wind.